"You could do something during the Rodeo Days," I suggest. "Be in the parade. Wear a really outrageous costume."

Charlotte thinks about it for a few minutes, then says, "I know. How about if I *don't* wear a costume? How about if I streak naked down the street?" she asks, just as Steve comes up to the table with our platters of eggs and pancakes.

Steve obviously overhears, because his hand wobbles as he tries to put our plates down. The sunny-side-down eggs that Charlotte ordered slither off the plate onto the table, nearly skidding into my lap. One of the yolks breaks and spreads slightly, but it's stopped by a hardened ridge of syrup on the table that holds it in, like a dam. All that's between me and Steve now is an egg moat.

CATHERINE CLARK

Better Latte Than Never

HARPER TEEN
An Imprint of HarperCollinsPublishers

HarperTeen is an imprint of HarperCollins Publishers.

Better Latte Than Never
Copyright © 2003 by Catherine Clark
All rights reserved. Printed in the United States of America. No part of this
book may be used or reproduced in any manner whatsoever without written
permission except in the case of brief quotations embodied in critical articles
and reviews. For information address HarperCollins Children's Books, a
division of HarperCollins Publishers, 1350 Avenue of the Americas, New
York, NY 10019.

www.harperteen.com

Library of Congress catalog card number: 2007929411
ISBN 978-0-06-136714-4

Typography by Alison Donalty
❖
Revised edition, 2008

For my father

Acknowledgments

I'd like to thank Abby McAden for helping me see this through from first fragments to finished manuscript, and Jill Grinberg for her support along the way. Many thanks to Keith Wood for brainstorming with me, and to Ellen, Annita, and everyone else in the Tattered Cover A/R Department for talking about bus drivers one morning.

Contents

Better Latte Than Never

Coffee Wench

It's my fifth day of summer vacation and I'm about to be killed by a Doberman.

This isn't the way I would have chosen to go. Having my legs gnawed off, just because I have to skate to work at Gas 'n Git. No one else is out here at 5:30 in the morning; no one will find me until after 6:00. I'll bleed to death from multiple puncture wounds. I'll come down with rabies and froth at the mouth, like a human cappuccino machine.

The dog charges out of his yard, high jumping the fence, when he sees me coming down the street. Then he races behind me, trying to nip at my heels. I don't know why he'd want to do that, unless he's not fond of his teeth. These heels are dangerously large; there are wheels attached to them.

Where is this dog's owner? Where are the dog police?

I try to decide whether I should brake and scare him with the loud noise of my screeching worn-out rubber heel, or whether I should speed skate to the end of the block, but that's probably impossible because there are so many large cracks in the sidewalk that I'd end up flat on my face. All I know is that this dog wants to kill me. Or just maim me, maybe. This is the third day in a row he's pursued me like I'm breakfast.

I can't skate down the other side of the street, because there's no sidewalk over there. I'd take another route, but there are no other routes—unless I go about five miles out of my way, which I'm not doing at 5:30 A.M. I probably shouldn't even be out here this early by myself, but it's the only way I can get to work and I have to work mornings because this is the only shift I can get at the only job I can get.

The phrase *running out of options* comes to mind.

The phrase *pepper spray* also comes to mind.

There must be a town ordinance against this. Even *Lindville* has standards for keeping dogs from killing innocent girls on in-line skates.

Suddenly the Doberman loses interest in me and runs back toward his yard, jumping back over the fence.

I adjust my courier bag and helmet and focus on the street again. Another day, another near death by Doberman. This is the type of summer I've always dreamed of.

Later that morning, I'm standing behind the counter at Espress-Oh-Yes when the world's worst coffee breath walks in.

I've only been working here for three days and already I recognize him, a guy in a pinstriped suit who is as jittery as a hummingbird. He is tense, he drives a silver Lexus and parks next to the side door in a No Parking area, and he orders the Premium Morning Blend, Tanker size, at about 6:50 A.M. Then he comes back later, intermittently, throughout the day, the way headaches do sometimes.

I work at a mini coffee shop that's inside a gas station, so all of the sizes are linked to the automotive world: Coupe, Sedan, SUV, Tanker. The coffee machines are shaped like gas tanks. They have pumps and little black rubber hoses that dispense hot beverages instead of flammable liquids. I wear an apron that has a black-and-white checkered-flag pattern, and a red plastic name tag that's shaped like a sports car.

It's just one more reminder that I'm not allowed to drive. My parents confiscated my license a few months ago, because I had two accidents and totaled the station wagon that they gave me when they bought a new sedan for my father's realty business. I'm spending my summer paying them back for all the auto body work over the past year. My parents say they don't trust me, and their insurance rates are through the roof, and would be even higher if they kept me on the policy. "You've become too much of a liability," my father told me as he stashed my license somewhere in his desk.

Let me tell you. There's nothing more annoying than

3

working at a coffee shop inside a gas station—and not being able to drive. Especially when you want to drive far, far away from here.

I pour the guy's coffee and shuffle him down to the cash register, inhaling deeply and then holding my breath, which is hard to do when you're supposed to greet the customer and tell him how much he owes. Good thing I have a lot of practice at holding my breath, because our town smells pretty bad sometimes, due to having some extremely large cattle feedlots nearby. We actually have an "odor hotline" here in Lindville, and some days the phone has to be ringing off the hook. The combination of manure and slaughterhouse aromas makes this a very fragrant place to live.

"One forty-nine," I say, then I stop breathing again, close off all intake valves: nose, mouth, even skin. Close the pores! Like it's a ship or a sub going down. Batten down the hatches. Whatever *batten* means. It sounds like a mistake I'd make on a vocabulary test; the past tense of *to bat*.

"What do you think of the nice bright sunshine this morning!" Coffee Breath says.

"Mm," I say as I hand him his change and he drops two quarters in the tip cup. "It's, um, nice. And bright." Exactly. *Do not inhale, do not inhale*, I tell myself.

"You know what? I think we're in for a long, hot summer. I guess we'll be switching to iced coffee pretty soon, right?" He laughs as he puts the top on his Tanker.

4

Either iced coffee or an oxygen mask, I think. His laughing expels a lot of breath, proving once again that he drinks coffee at home before he comes here. I take a huge step back and nearly trip on the black rubber floor mat.

"Take care, see you later!" he calls as he heads for the door.

"Thanks, good-bye!" I breathe deeply. Finally. Oxygen. I drink a shot of cold water to try to clear out the porous cells in my throat. It's a curse to have such a heightened sense of smell, it really is.

We have this jar next to the cash register and it's piled high with fruit candies and mints, just for people like him. But he won't take one, will he? He just drives off to wherever he goes every day, where he can torture more people with his breath.

Fortunately, there's a lull and I sort of collapse against the wall as I wait for the next customer. I need time to recover. I wish the truck driver who wears strong cologne and always has minty-fresh breath would come in.

"So what horrible thing did you do to end up here?" the boy behind the cash register asks me as I push back my hair and retie my Espress-Oh-Yes apron. He rings up car washes and bottled soda, reads music magazines from the store newsstand, and turns up the store radio really loud whenever a U2 song comes on—if our manager's gone, that is. He's usually so busy reading or writing in a notebook that he doesn't talk to me. He's lucky because he

5

doesn't have to wear the checkered-flag apron—just a red polo shirt with the Gas 'n Git logo.

"What are you talking about? I didn't do anything," I say.

I think he's trying to look like Bono, but he just isn't that good-looking. I'm sorry, but it's true. He's wearing blue-tinted plastic glasses like Bono's and has longish brown hair brushed back like Bono's. But he's got a crooked nose and I think he's trying to grow a mustache. I'm not sure, though—it could just be lint. Doesn't he realize that Bono is mustache free? Or is he going for the stubble look? Anyway, the Gas 'n Git polo shirt seriously interferes with this attempted rock-star look.

"Come on," he says, and I can swear I hear a slight, fake Irish accent in his voice. "Give me a break. You've got to have a story. People don't end up working here without a story."

He's right. I do have a story. But I'm wondering, if that's true, then what is *his* story? I've never seen him around town, until I got this job. He seems too old for high school, but only by about a year. So where did he come from? What's *he* doing here?

"Well, if you're not going to share the details, then could you at least explain your name tag? Are there typos? Because I don't think I'm reading it right," he says.

"It's Fleming."

"Fleming?" He can't quite comprehend it. Most people

can't. "Is that your first name or your last name?"

"First," I say. I don't bother to explain that it's my middle name—that I was named for Peggy Fleming, the American figure skater who dazzled the world wearing chartreuse and won a gold medal in the 1968 Winter Olympics. Peggy Fleming inspired my father to get into ice skating, so he named me after her. And then he was on a roll with the concept and decided to give my brother and sisters figure skaters' names, too: Torvill and Dean, the almost-five-year-old twins, and then there's my little sister Dorothy Hamill Farrell, who's three. My mother is pregnant again, and who knows what name they'll choose this time.

Some people think these skaters' names are really cute—like my parents and grandparents—but I don't. It's really hard to walk around with an Olympic champion's name. People tend to expect things of you, and if you don't deliver . . .

Also, nobody else my age has the name *Peggy*.

No offense, Peggy Fleming. My dad, Phil Farrell, creator of the not-so-famous Farrell Flip, still worships you, and I think you're incredible, too. And no offense to all the other Peggys, or Peggies, of the world. I just don't *feel* like a Peggy.

I also don't look anything like Peggy Fleming. We're complete opposites. She has beautiful long brown hair and blue eyes. She's petite and graceful. She's a gorgeous, artistic skater, and a very knowledgeable and entertaining commentator.

Me? I have long, wavy sandy blond hair, green eyes, freckles, I'm five foot eight, and I haven't ice skated well—or much at all—since the eighth grade. Enough said.

"Fleming. Interesting," the guy says. "Anyone ever call you phlegmball?"

"No," I say. "But thanks for asking."

He frowns at me. "Do you go to Franklin?"

"No," I say.

"Oh. So you go to Edison?" he asks.

"Yes," I say.

He stares at me for a minute and is starting to look irritated. "You know, you're incredibly talkative. People really love that in a coffee wench. I bet you'll score lots of tips. Oh, yeah. You'll be rich in no time."

I don't answer him.

"Well, thanks for asking, Fleming. My name's Denny," he says. "But my best friends call me Perkins."

I smile. "Really?"

"I was just kidding," he says as he takes a customer's credit card.

I decide to ignore his joke, even though it is sort of funny. "Where do *you* go to school?" I ask.

"I'm between schools," he says.

This sounds interesting. I've heard of being between

jobs, and between boyfriends. But between schools? Is he taking a year off? Or was he kicked out? "Well, where *did* you go to school?" I ask.

"I'm a proud graduate of New Horizons Day Care," Denny says. "After that it all went downhill and turned into a bland mix of study halls and very scarring marching-band experiences." He shudders, making a face.

"You? Marching band? I can't picture it," I say.

"Neither could I. Quit the Franklin Mustangs' finest after freshman year," he says. "Started focusing on real bands. Now I write music. Well, not music exactly—songs. Lyrics. And some poetry." He pushes a strand of hair behind his ear.

The gas station poet, I think. Great. Does he write epics about unleaded? "So . . . are you ever going back to school?" I ask.

"I took the last year off, after graduating. I'm supposed to start college this fall," Denny says, "but I don't know if I'll go."

"Really? Why not?" I ask.

"Do I *need* classes?" Denny shrugs. "I don't know. I think I'm doing okay on my own."

"Working here is okay?" I ask. In what universe? I'm about to ask him where he's going to college when the place gets really busy again.

I'm starting to get into the rhythm of the espresso machine when Mr. Stinson, owner of Western Wear

Bonanza in the mall, comes in. Despite the heat, he's wearing corduroy pants and a beige wool cardigan sweater with wood buttons that look like Brazil nuts. It's like he's never really left England. Mr. Stinson has terrible vision, even with his giant tortoiseshell glasses on. Maybe he won't see that it's me, I think. Maybe the obnoxious apron will distract him.

I keep my head down. "What would you like this morning?" I mumble.

"Yes, hello, I'd like . . ." Mr. Stinson is about to order when he realizes that it's me standing behind the Muffins of the Month. "You," he says, glowering at me.

"Hello, Mr. Stinson," I say politely. "How are you?"

"What is the likes of you doing here?" he asks.

It's a long story, I think. *And you know part of it.* "What can I get you?" I ask, still trying to be friendly.

"Well, now, let's see. How about if we start off with a check to pay for the damage you did to my store window? And then perhaps you could return the belt you stole, and the leather bag . . . well, the list goes on, doesn't it?"

"I didn't steal anything," I say. "I bought all those things with my employee discount—"

"Which I never should have extended to you. It was a privilege, not a right. Do you understand the difference, young lady? And then there's the small matter of a smashed window."

"Um . . . I thought your insurance covered that," I say.

"There's a little *item* in insurance called a *deductible*. I don't know if they bother to teach you that word in dreadful American high schools, but the word is *deductible*."

I want to fire wooden stir sticks at Mr. Stinson. Do I know the word *deductible*? It's why I'm working here—it's why I'm standing here asking for his coffee order.

But Mr. Stinson and I have had this argument a few times before, so I decide to move on. "So. Would you like some tea this morning?" I ask.

"Do you know, you absolutely ruined my Christmas season." Mr. Stinson's bushy eyebrows are twitching in time to the song on the radio. "You left me high and dry. You—oh, never mind, my blood pressure's high enough without this—without coffee—without seeing *you*. In the future, I'll find somewhere else to purchase my petrol." He shakes his head and grabs a bottle of juice, heading for Denny's register, not even dealing with me.

As if I'm going to be so hurt that he won't fill his tank with our gas—excuse me—*petrol*.

After he leaves, Denny turns to me with a sort of smirk on his face. "So. That's how you ended up here."

"What?" I say.

"*You're* the one who sent the bronc-riding Santa Claus mannequin flying into his store window," Denny says. "I saw that in the newspaper."

Not much happens here, yet I've been in two *Lindville Gazette* headlines so far, and I'm only sixteen.

11

Denny nods. "Impressive. But what was the bit about the stolen leather items?"

"I didn't steal anything," I tell him.

"Come on, Fleming. Face facts. You're a shoplifter with a leather fetish. Just admit it. You know, because once you own up to it, you can get help."

"I didn't shoplift, and I'm not into leather!" I protest.

"Then what was he talking about?"

"It's a long story."

"Uh-huh. That's what they all say." Denny is trying to build what looks like a log cabin out of rolls of peppermint Mentos.

"Who says that?" I mutter.

"Hey, this place is a *haven* for former offenders, don't worry," Denny says. "Kelly? Hacked into computers. Rick? Embezzled money from a bank. And our manager, the fair Jamie? Guilty of identity theft. She screwed up, though, and chose a really bad identity."

"You're joking, right?" I say. "You *are* joking."

Denny's house of Mentos collapses and a couple roll off the counter to the floor. "Only a little," he says as he picks them up and puts them back into the display rack.

"What about you? What's your offense?" I ask. *Besides that thing you call a mustache and the fact you're putting floor-lint-covered candy back on the rack.*

"I have done nothing," Denny says. "I'm just here to counterbalance the rest of you people. But let's just say we'll be counting the coffee beans from now on, okay? And I for one will be keeping a closer eye on my wallet, not to mention my cash drawer."

I glare at his black leather wallet, which is hanging on a metal chain from his pocket. Denny rides a motorcycle and thinks that gives him dispensation to wear certain kinds of clothes and accessories.

"Don't worry," I tell him. "I'm not interested in your wallet. Believe me."

"That's what they all say." Denny swings his wallet around like a lariat. He grins as he walks toward me. The metal chain catches on a drawer handle and nearly rips the belt loop off his jeans.

"This is all your fault," he says, trying to unjam the metal chain. "You're one of those bad-luck kind of people, aren't you?"

"Oh, yeah. I'm cursed or something," I say.

Actually, that isn't far from the truth.

How Am I Driving?

I get off of work at noon. It's only six hours, but it seems like the longest shift ever, maybe because it starts at 6:00 A.M. I've been smelling and serving coffee all morning, and I'm thinking I may never drink coffee again. Which is all right; I've never liked it that much—I mostly just drink it at IHOP because of the refillable pitcher. And a certain waiter.

"There comes a time when everyone has to make sacrifices," my dad said when we talked about me taking the Espress-Oh-Yes job. "And you have reached that time, P. F."

Other sacrifices in my life: I look after my siblings a couple of mornings a week, the days I'm not working at Gas 'n Git, while my mom's at the radio station and my dad's figure skating. That's just the scheduled summer baby-sitting. That doesn't count the other times I know I'll be called on to help. And I have to turn over almost all of the money I'm making to my parents because I owe them for the car repairs.

I'm taking the bus to French class, starting today, because of that certain IHOP waiter and because I can graduate early if I get ahead on my credits. I want to travel for a while before going away to college. I'd love to go to France and actually *use* my French, but since I probably won't be able to afford it, I'll start out just cruising around the States, checking out places I've been before and places I haven't. My parents and I used to travel a lot, before we settled here. I was a world traveler, or at least a U.S. traveler, until I turned six. It's very sad to contemplate that my life was more exciting as a toddler than it is now. I try not to think about it. I try to focus on getting out of debt and hitting the road.

Of course, for that I'll need a car. Which is also why I'm *here*, this summer, not working as a camp counselor like my best friend, Suzanne. It's all about paying my parents back.

I look up at the bus-stop sign, which has our town's motto on it: LINDVILLE IS KINDVILLE——BE A GOOD NEIGHBOR! DON'T LITTER. There should be a garbage can next to the sign, but there isn't. That figures.

At school we have different versions of the town slogan carved into the desks and written on lockers, including: Lindville is Kind-a-lame-ville, Lindville is Stinkville, and Lindville Sucks.

All I know is that it will be a happy day when I see that

"Lindville is Kindville" sign in my rearview mirror.

Because it will mean two things: one, I am actually driving a car again, and two, I am leaving Lindville for greener pastures. Which won't be difficult to find, because we mostly just have brown pastures here.

At 12:06 I see the Lindvillager, precisely on schedule, coming down the street. Lindville's not big enough to have actual bus-size buses—we have the short kind, the type that you ride on at an airport when you catch a car-rental shuttle.

The town had a contest to come up with a cute name for the bus system when they started it a few years ago. "Lindvillager" is the best they could do. The bus has fake wood trim, like it's an old-fashioned station wagon. Unfortunately, the paintings of the cute little village on the side got obscured by giant ads for radio stations and restaurants, and just recently those got removed and replaced by a huge ad for July's big annual event, the Lindville Rodeo Roundup Days—as if we could forget they're coming in July.

The pseudo-bus pulls up in front of me with a screech. When the door opens, I see it's Kamikaze Bus Driver again. This guy has this route nearly every day, which worries me.

He has no sense of speed limits. He constantly cuts in front of cars. He merges without even glancing in his side mirror. He takes off when a passenger's foot is barely off the bottom step. He's a Driver's Ed *Don't*. You know those "How Am I Driving?" stickers they put on trucks? Now I know why they don't put them on Lindville's buses.

If my parents knew this was the person driving me around town, they would give me back my license and a car so fast it would make even Kamikaze Bus Driver's head spin. Only I'm not sure if it could spin, because he has so much gray hair on his face and neck and such a long beard that it might choke him. He wears a peace-sign button on his lapel every day, and occasionally adds another sixties memento to his outfit via wristband or headband. The back of his uniform shirt constantly has this wet trail of sweat down the middle of it, which, unfortunately, is something you notice when you sit behind a person.

There's this sign over his head that says, **YOUR DRIVER:** _____. **PROFESSIONAL & COURTEOUS**. Kamikaze Bus Driver won't fill in his name, because if we don't know his name, we can't complain about things, like how two days ago he raced across a railroad crossing to beat an oncoming freight train, right as the bar was lowering.

But the *really* sad part is, that's probably the most exciting thing that's happened to me so far this summer.

I have hope, though. For some strange reason, I have hope.

I take a seat behind an elderly woman with a laundry bag, and in front of a guy with brown hair and a mustache, tight Wrangler jeans, and a T-shirt that says, **FORGET THE WHALES, SAVE THE COWBOYS**!

I always sort of wonder how other people end up on the bus. Not that it's a bad thing; just a curious thing around here, because most people seem to have their 2.7 cars per household, no matter what shape they or the cars are in. People just *drive*, and if they can't, they get someone else to drive them. I think there are more gas stations per capita here than in any other town or city in the country. Hence the fact that I can get employed at Gas 'n Git. People need gas; gas stations need warm bodies to run them.

Me? I'm on the bus because a week after I got my license in November, I crashed while turning into the Happy Hamburger parking lot. Happy Hamburger is the most popular lunch place for our school. You would think we wouldn't want to eat burgers, since we drive past so many cattle in feedlots every day, but no, it's like there's something in the air that makes you want beef, because you don't want to let the town down or something. We have to make sure the meat business thrives, because that's where our parents' jobs are, and if it dies, we all die with it.

Anyway, that day freezing rain was falling and the streets were icy and I turned left while accelerating, which I found out later you're not supposed to do, and the car started to skid. I couldn't remember which direction to steer, whether to brake or not, so the car just kept sliding sideways. First we knocked over the giant brown plastic steer out front. Then we skidded right up to the Happy Hamburger and fishtailed right into the building.

Everyone from school was inside, either in line or eating. Everyone *saw* us. It was so embarrassing.

But then this amazing thing happened. Steve Gropher, who I didn't even know then, came running outside to see if I was okay. Well, technically he could have been coming to check on Suzanne and her ex-boyfriend Rick, who were in the car with me at the time, but he ran right over to *me*. He was there in about two seconds and he said he'd seen it happening because he looked up from the ketchup pump dispenser just in time.

I wasn't hurt, but I was in shock, and I kept saying, "Oh, God, I can't believe I just did that. Did I just do that? I can't believe I just did that," over and over, while he sat there next to me and someone called an ambulance and a tow truck and my parents. We were all fine—just some cuts and bruises—but everyone thought I was bleeding profusely because Steve had been clutching those little paper cups of ketchup when he ran outside and they'd gotten crushed in his hand and spilled all over both of us when he hugged me and tried to calm me down.

I didn't know Steve then, because he had only moved to Lindville that fall. All I knew about him was that he was a junior like me, he was a waiter at IHOP, and that he was very good-looking. So that was my happy accident, if there is such a thing.

As far as my vehicular career goes, things went downhill after that. Of course, my parents wanted me to get a job so I could pay them back for the one-thousand-dollar deductible they had to spend to get the car fixed up. All the good jobs were taken, but I got this Christmas-season job working for Mr. Stinson at Western Wear Bonanza. He was trying to drum up business, so he rented this mechanical bull called "Rudy the Red-Nosed Rein-Steer." If people could stay on the bull for fifteen seconds, then they got to choose a "Bonanza Bonus," which was a cheesy free gift, like a bumper sticker or a bandana.

It turned out that no one could stay on the bull very long. There are plenty of real, authentic, hardworking cowboys around here who could have stayed on for hours, and had enough left afterward to kick Mr. Stinson all the way to the food court. But most of them don't shop at the Sunset Mall, so instead we got a lot of suburban customers with no skill.

I was working the night shift one Saturday when Suzanne and some other friends from school came by. We were joking around, and I thought it would be funny if I put the store's Santa Claus mannequin on the bull and let Santa ride for a while.

It *was* funny. Very, very funny.

Until I turned the speed on the mechanical bull up too high, and Santa went flying off the rein-steer and into the left-side front window of the store. The glass cracked and Santa landed facedown on Mr. Stinson's "A Proper English Christmas" display, wrecking the plum pudding.

Needless to say, Mr. Stinson fired me. "You are a retailer's nightmare," he said. "Have you no concept of responsibility? Move on, Miss Farrell, move *on*. I never want to see you again. Not even as a customer. You are a bad seed," Mr. Stinson said. "A very, very bad seed."

Needless to say, Mr. Stinson is a little over the top. I didn't like working for him and I was actually okay with losing the job.

A couple of weeks later, I went to work for Bob's Pizza. They didn't care about my retail history, but they maybe should have checked into my driving record. I'm not sure I need to really go into it. Let's just say that it involved a desperate attempt to match the competition and deliver pizza in thirty minutes or less.

I totaled the car that had just been repaired. My father gave me some lecture about making the same mistake twice. My parents donated the banged-up station wagon to charity. And now I take the bus.

So, I guess you could say that I don't do well with steering—or steers. Part of the reason I took the job inside Gas 'n Git is that I thought it might bring me good karma, spending time around gas pumps and helping people in cars. If there's a fuel god, I'll pray to him or her. It can't hurt.

The Lindvillager pulls up in front of the school. As I start to get off the bus, Kamikaze Bus Driver puts his hand on my arm. "Excuse me, miss," he says. His voice sounds like tires on a gravel road. In the rain.

"Um, hi," I say, pulling my arm away from him.

"Next time you work at the gas station—tomorrow?" he asks in a gruff voice, his words emerging from the curly beard in a muffle. He doesn't take off his octagon-shaped sunglasses.

"No, not until next Monday."

"Okay, then. Monday. Bring me a large coffee." He shoves a couple of dollars at me.

The last thing this man needs is more caffeine, I think. But okay, whatever he says. My life can't get weird enough. Now I'm taking coffee orders from insane bus drivers.

I have to get out of this town.

En français, s'il vous plaît

On the blackboard there's a sentence: *C'est le premier jour de la plus de votre vie*.

"Today is the first day of the rest of your life." Or something like that. *En français*.

Actually I think it's the first day of Intermediate Semi-Accelerated-Because-It's-Summer French. Monday, Wednesday, Thursday, 12:30–2:00.

I take a seat, and right away a girl who was walking across the school lawn beside me takes a seat next to me. We exchange awkward smiles. She has perfectly straight, long reddish hair and is wearing a purple tank top with a washed-out silver crown on it. I don't know her, and I'm guessing she goes to Franklin. This is a combination summer school at Edison High, for students from all over the region. The teacher from Franklin, Monsieur LeFleur, is supposed to be excellent. Everyone raves about him, about how he makes crepes and teaches the geography of

France with travel videos.

I glance up at the clock. It's 12:30. Where's Steve Gropher?

To take French—or any foreign language—in Lindville in the summer seems very bizarre. This feels about as far away from France as you can get. We're sitting in a hot classroom with the windows open, it's ninety degrees outside, and the hot wind is blowing smells from the rendering plant into the room. If you've never smelled a rendering plant, it's sort of like spoiled, canned cat food that's been left out in the sun to bake. Not that I've ever had a cat, but that's what other people say.

This kind of situation isn't exactly covered in phrase books. *Comment est-ce qu'on dit?*: "It smells like death today"?

I glance at the clock again. Now it's 12:35. Where's Steve? And where's Monsieur LeFleur?

A woman enters the classroom a few minutes later and quickly takes roll. This doesn't make sense, unless Monsieur LeFleur is running late, or unless he is too brilliant to take roll and has someone else do it for him—a French secretary. Except that she doesn't sound or look French. She's wearing an American-flag T-shirt with a styleless khaki skirt and blue sandals.

I look around the classroom as I hear names called. Steve said he was going to take French this summer, too. I could have sworn he said he'd be in this class. We talked about it a couple of times. But he's a no show. He's not even on the class list. I can't believe he blew it off. I recognize a few other people in the room from Edison, but I only know them vaguely.

"Good news, class," the woman says after finishing roll. "Your teacher, Monsieur LeFleur, is ill today."

People around me start high-fiving each other, and then the woman says, "Therefore, you will be doing quiet reading of your textbook for one hour, and then I will give you a quiz."

"So what was the *good* news?" the red-haired girl next to me asks. "Did I miss something?"

The woman frowns at her. "The good news is that you might have gotten out earlier than usual if you hadn't just been so rude." She clears her throat and looks at her list. "Your name is, again? *En français, s'il vous plaît.*"

"How can I say my name in French?" the girl asks.

"You know what I mean," the woman says. "Introduce yourself, *en français.*"

"*Jeu mappel* Charlotte Duncan," the girl says in a flat accent as she cracks her gum.

"Charlotte. No gum chewing in French class."

"Don't French people chew gum?" Charlotte asks.

A few people laugh and the woman clears her throat. "The point is that you will be working on pronunciation in this class. *You* will be working on it especially hard. Gum and candy interfere with this important step. But

25

never mind, for now—begin reading. I am sure that Monsieur LeFleur will be here for your next class. He has not had a sick day in eight years."

I crack open my textbook, and Charlotte leans over toward my desk. "How do you say 'bad air day' *en français?*"

"Je m'appelle Lindville," I say, and we laugh. It sort of makes up for Steve not being here. Sort of.

Rooty Tooty, What a Cutie

"So what are you up to now?" Charlotte asks me as we're dismissed from class. Even though I just met her, for some reason I confide in Charlotte and tell her I want to go to IHOP after class. I tell her that it isn't because it's international and it isn't because it's a house and it isn't because of the pancakes, though they are an excellent side benefit. I explain there's this waiter I know, who I kind of want to see, who was supposed to be in French with us. I don't know why I'm telling her all of this. Pouring my heart out isn't something I usually do. But she's just so easy to talk to that before I know what I'm doing, I've confessed my need for an IHOP fix.

"The waiter's a friend of yours?" she asks.

"Sort of," I say.

"You like him." She nods knowingly. "Let's go."

I'm so glad she's going with me. Going alone seems sort of pathetic, although I was willing to do it.

IHOP is very close to Edison High, which means it's a huge school hangout. It's only a ten-minute walk, but no one ever actually *walks* there. It's just not done. Unless you're me, and you can't drive, and you have a desperate need to get to IHOP. Then you walk. It's a horrible walk, but it's my favorite one.

Charlotte and I make small talk as we wait for a light to change so we can sprint across the street. There isn't a crosswalk and there's never a light for pedestrians. That's just the way it is here.

We walk past prairie dogs in a vacant lot on the side of the road, perched atop dirt mounds, chirping to each other. They've taken over fields like this all over town, and they keep building new colonies and growing in number, despite the fact that they're constantly getting run over when they try to cross the road to other, more vacant lots.

It's windy and a few small tumbleweeds blow across the breakdown lane ahead of us as we hike through the brown dirt on the side of the road. So much dust is in the air that my eyes keep watering. The good thing about the wind is that it's now blowing hard in an easterly direction, and the feedlot odors are blowing out of Lindville and into the next town. We export our bad air. Sort of the way World's Worst Coffee Breath exports his bad air into Gas 'n Git.

I glance up at the billboard hovering over us. There's a painting of a giant black bull, with the initials IZ branded into his flank, facing down a couple of grinning rodeo clowns. DON'T MISS INSANE ZANE! LINDVILLE RODEO ROUNDUP DAYS—JULY 10–JULY 20. LASSO YOUR TICKETS TODAY! it says in loopy, brown rope-style script.

When we first moved here, back when I was six, I thought this was so cool. I couldn't wait to go. I watched the big parade, I cruised the petting zoo, I begged my parents to take me on rides every day, I ate a pork chop on a stick, I had a riding lesson and got my picture taken with a cowboy. I loved everything about Rodeo Roundup Days.

Now, it just seems sort of worn out and maybe a little sad. The parade with longhorn cattle, town officials waving to the crowd from pickup truck beds, and marching bands wilting in their heavy uniforms in the summer heat. The bucking bronco contests and the side show of "Amazing Farm Animals." The carnival rides with the jaded, inattentive operators who chew tobacco and spit the juice on the hot pavement—and occasionally hit my shoe, like one did last summer.

"You know what? I think that Village Inn pancakes are better than IHOP's," Charlotte says as she kicks an empty beer can out of her way. "I think actually that maybe they're exactly the *same*, but at Village Inn maybe you're expecting less, so you're not disappointed, whereas a place that brags about pancakes—well, you know, they have a higher standard to live up to. And living up to standards is like . . ."

"The worst," I say. Does she know what it's like to have a former competitive figure skater for a dad? And a meteorologist mom who can predict the temperature every day to within one degree?

"Exactly," Charlotte says as she dodges a flying taco wrapper being whipped along by the wind. My mom would know precisely how strong the wind is, but I'll just say "very strong."

At IHOP, there's a young, blond hostess I don't recognize, who tries to seat us by the bathroom. We insist on a booth by the window. Steve's tables are usually in this area, but as soon as we sit down, I notice that he's across the restaurant, working on the other side of the hostess station. I try not to take this as a sign of things to come.

Seeing Steve, I completely forget about everything else that happened today. Good, bad, indifferent—it doesn't matter. Rooty tooty, what a cutie. He's about six feet tall, which is important when you're five foot eight like me. He has short, spiky blond hair and blue eyes, and a scar on his cheek that he got from jumping off a house roof in fourth grade and landing on a tree. He has another scar, on his knee, from where a car hit him when he was riding a bike.

Maybe I like him so much because we're both so accident prone. And he doesn't like his name, either—he even stole my idea and used his middle name, wearing a "Josh" name tag at IHOP for a few months.

Steve can beat almost anyone at pool, and there was a rumor going around school that he was in a 12-step program for a gambling addiction. Don't ask me why that's cool, but it is. Steve's lived in a few different cities, the way I used to, the way I wish I still could sometimes, except then he wouldn't be in any of those places, so what would be the point? He has a dozen plans for getting out of Lindville when he graduates. He works as many hours as he can here, even on Saturday nights, because he's saving all his money to go on this cross-country trip, which he's going to do the day after graduation.

Whenever we hang out, we always talk about the places we'd rather be, or want to visit, or live in, and we always sort of talk about it like it's something we could do together, if we weren't stuck in Lindville celebrating the sports event or holiday *du jour*. Like the way we talked about both taking French so we could go AWOL on the spring class trip to Montreal.

Instead of Steve, someone named Roger who I've also never seen here before takes our order. Roger wears large square glasses and looks about forty years old.

"That's not the guy. Is it?" Charlotte asks once he's gone. "Please tell me that's not the guy."

"No, that's not him!" I start laughing, forgetting Charlotte doesn't know me yet and I have to explain. So I do. I tell her about how I met Steve, how we kissed a few times, how I keep hoping we'll go out.

I don't tell her the stupid things. Like how, because Steve was a new guy in town, I decided that must mean he was The One. I don't tell her how, the first time Steve and I kissed, on New Year's Eve, he whispered in my ear, "I can't believe I just did that. Did I just do that? I can't believe I just did that," teasing me about how we first met and how freaked out I was. I don't tell Charlotte how happy that made me, because it was the best thing that had happened to me in so long, and that I thought my new year was off to this incredible start. I don't tell her that the next time I saw Steve, at school, he acted like it had never happened. Because I could handle being the New-Year's-fling girl. Sort of.

We kissed again on February 15. He was a day late for being my Valentine. We were working on this heinous group history project for school, and decided it would be more fun to ditch the group and make out instead.

The last time we kissed was when he rescued me at a St. Patrick's Day party. This guy who was either carried away by the love of the Irish—I do have green eyes and a few freckles—or the cups of green beer would not leave me alone. I don't even know who he was—someone's cousin, from another town. He kept trying to put his arms around me, and then he actually pulled me onto the sofa and I sort of screamed. Steve told the guy to get lost, and then he and I hung out on the porch for a while, and one thing led to the usual. He even ditched his friends at the party to walk me home, which seemed huge to me. No guy had ever walked me home before.

I don't know if his friends got mad at him, or what. But it's like ever since then, there's been this tension between us. Or at least, *I* feel tension, because he's acting like we're only friends and that's it, as if nothing ever happened, as if we haven't kissed and had these really intense conversations. I don't *get* it.

I have hope, though. We're due for another fling. It's been almost three months. We're overdue. If we were a library book, there would be a huge fine due on us.

I look across the restaurant at Steve, who's carrying a tray of beverages to a table of two middle-aged guys in overalls and baseball caps. Why does he have to wait on them and not me?

"French. Give me a break," Charlotte says, flipping through our textbook, glancing at the photographs. "I am not into summer school at all. You know? I'm only taking this class because I've gotta get the credit so I can graduate next year, because I'm behind in credits." She explains how she and her little sister and her mom have moved four times in the past five years due to job transfers.

"That sounds kind of hard," I say, although I'm a little envious, too.

Charlotte takes a sip of her water. "Yeah. It is. It's like—you just get to know people, and then you leave. But I get to meet tons of people, so . . ." She shrugs. "How about you? How long have you been here?"

"Forever." I tell her how we traveled around constantly when I was young because my father was competing and then performing as a professional figure skater. Then we settled down in Lindville when I was six. My dad got a job as a realtor, my mother became a radio meteorologist, they decided to have the big family they'd always wanted, and we haven't been anywhere fun in years.

"So wait a second," she says. "Your dad—he's like Brian Boitano or something?"

"Not quite. No gold medals," I say. "But he's good."

"Wow. That is so cool. I'd love to see him sometime. So hold on. Do you skate?" she asks.

"Not really," I say. "I mean, I used to, but then I quit."

"How come? God, I totally admire anyone who can do anything athletic," she says as Roger comes over and sets a syrup carousel on our table with absolutely zero flair.

"Your order will be right up," he tells us before vanishing into the kitchen.

I glance over at Steve. I have to go talk to him. This is the first time I've seen him since summer vacation started.

"So you're taking French. What else? Are you working?" Charlotte asks me.

I nod. "At the coffee place Espress-Oh-Yes—you know where the Gas 'n Git station is, on Highway eighty-seven? Inside there."

"Hey, that's cool," Charlotte says.

"Not really," I tell her. "I have to be there before six in the morning, and I have this coworker who thinks he's Bono."

"Oh, yeah? Well, I work at Shady Prairies," she says.

"You're kidding," I say. Shady Prairies is a huge, new retirement apartment complex on the east side of town. When they put it in five years ago, they took down a lot of old trees to make room for pools and a golf course. If there's any shade left, I'd be surprised. "What do you do there?" I ask.

"I work in the dining room—serving. It's sort of fun, actually—they have two seatings for dinner, at four-thirty and six, and then we're out of there by eight. The people are nice—most of them, anyway. They always want to know what I'm doing with my life. If I have direction. Then they tell me about these trips they took like fifty years ago, and how I've gotta get out and see the world before it's too late." She pauses and cracks her green-colored bubble gum. "Which is true."

I look over at Steve bringing a tray of food to a table. As I watch him, I make circles on the table with the blueberry syrup dispenser, but it keeps getting stuck to spilled syrup on the table.

"Oh." Charlotte looks up at Roger as he sets her plate in front of her. "Thanks."

I thank him, too, as Charlotte covers her pancakes with all four kinds of syrup and a packet of mixed-fruit jelly. She puts a dollop of ketchup on the side of her plate, as if she's thinking of dipping later.

I stare past her at Steve, who's joking around with a table of police officers. He really has a rapport with the regulars here.

Charlotte taps her fork against my plate to get my attention. "So, that's him?" She gestures behind her with her fork.

I nod. "Sorry. Was that way too obvious?"

"He's cute. Go say hi," Charlotte urges me. "Ask him why he's not suffering through French with us."

"Really? Should I do that?" I ask. "I don't know, though. Do you think I should? I mean, my pancakes are going to get cold."

"Like you're going to eat them if you don't go say hi. What do you have to lose, anyway? Go for it," she says.

Charlotte's attitude is so different from Suzanne's. Suzanne is usually telling me to hang back and wait for him to make a move. That hasn't exactly been working too well.

I set my napkin on the table and brush off my khakis. I wish they weren't so crinkled, but hey, it's been a long time since 5:00 A.M., when I got dressed. As I walk across the half-empty restaurant, I try to think of something witty to say, something that will impress him. First I see Steve perching on the end of a booth bench. I wonder who he's talking to—probably some more of his regular mid-afternoon customers. I can't see because of the wall partition separating that section.

Then I get closer and I see who he's sitting with. He has his arm around this beautiful girl who has an IHOP uniform on and I realize it's the new blond hostess and they're kissing.

He's not taking French class with me. He's Frenching some other girl.

I stand there for a second, doing my prairie-dog-in-headlights look, unable to move. I stare at her name tag: JACQUI. I wonder what kind of name that is, what kind of spelling that is. Meanwhile, JACQUI and Steve don't even notice I'm standing there.

And while before, I just *thought* this was shaping up to be the worst summer of my entire life? Now I know it's true.

"Hey, so what did he say?" Charlotte asks when I go back to our booth.

"I don't know," I say, sitting down with a squeak of vinyl. "I mean, nothing. He was with this girl. The hostess."

"What do you mean, he was with her?"

"They're making out," I tell Charlotte.

"What? No way." She sounds indignant. Charlotte cranes her neck to see them. She can't, so she stands up and half walks over to them, taking a few extra napkins off a service cart to give her trip purpose. "That girl looks like she's made out of plastic," she says when she comes back. "Did you see that nose job? And her hair color is *definitely* not natural."

I try to smile, because I appreciate what Charlotte's doing. But it doesn't really matter who the girl is. It just matters that Steve wants to kiss her and not me.

Weather on the Nines

At 6:45 A.M. I wander into the kitchen and my little sister Torvill is clamoring, "You're up, you're up, you're up!" She says things in threes now—it's her phase *du jour*, or rather, *du summer*.

It's the first day this week that I don't have to be at Gas 'n Git by 6:00. Dad just woke me on his way out, and Torvill, Dean, and Dorothy want their breakfasts. Mom is at the radio station to do her morning forecasts. I've got to watch the kids for the next four hours, until Dad gets home. Three mornings a week—and whenever else he can find time—he drives to an arena that is open year-round for serious figure skaters. He has a Russian coach named Ludmila, and he's trying to get up to speed so he can go on some Masters of Skating tour.

"Come on, you guys," I say, "don't you want to go back to bed? I think it's raining. Isn't it raining?"

I glance at Dorothy, who is sitting in the middle of the

kitchen floor, making a perfect, tall stack of plastic containers, in descending size. She'll be an engineer. She's brilliant and scientific that way.

Torvill runs over to the window. "It's sunny, it's sunny, it's sunny!"

"Then why do I hear water?" I ask.

"We were running water in the sink," Dean says. "Dad said to wash our hands."

I look at the kitchen sink, which is about to overflow. I rush over and turn it off, then pull the drain stopper free.

"Yogurt, yogurt, yogurt!" Torvill sings.

I rub my eyes as I look at her. Is it my imagination, or is her pink Barbie sleepwear suddenly a size too small for her?

Dean starts kicking the refrigerator. He wants to be a kickboxer, and thinks he should practice on every household item and anyone who's standing nearby.

I move Dean aside and get out the milk, yogurt, cereal, and fruit snacks. There's a note from Mom on the counter: "Peggy—Pears in Fridge, Please Use Up."

Like I want some aging, moldy pears for breakfast. They're not good enough for anyone else to use up, but they're okay for me? Or does she mean I should foist them on to the kids? It's unclear, like most of her early-morning notes. I want French toast, not pears. I want Eggs Benedict brought to me in bed, on a tray. In a fancy hotel. In a large city.

But no. I've got moldy pears and kids throwing cereal at me. And it's another fragrant Lindville morning.

We never should have traveled so much when I was young, because it makes me want more things than Lindville has. When I was born, my father was still competing as an amateur. But after he came in 4th at Nationals and then 8th and then 16th, he realized he was in a very bad trend, which could only eventually lead to 32nd, 64th and 128th. Not that they let that many skaters compete at Nationals, but you get the gist.

He had this move he created, called the Farrell Flip, where he held his hands a certain way on his hips when he did a flip jump. But it never really caught on the way the Salchow and the Axel did. He was never successful enough to end up on a cereal box, is what it boils down to.

So he decided to give up his Olympic dream and join an ice show. Starting from when I was two, we were on the road all the time, going from city to city, which might sound hard, but it was great. I met lots of people with really extreme makeup back then. I was only a toddler, so it couldn't have influenced me that much, but who knows? Maybe that's why I have such an aversion to eye shadow, and why I love staying in hotels and visiting new places. And why I hate being stuck in one place year after year.

When Dad got tired of skating in sweltering costumes, sometimes playing to big crowds, sometimes playing to empty rinks, occasionally crashing into the boards when he couldn't see out of his eyeholes, it was time for me to start school. We moved here because they both found jobs and we're close to my grandparents. But Dad still dreams of hearing Dick Button, former Olympic champion and a skating commentator for many years, talk about his marvelous power and spark and grace on the ice. I'm not sure Dick Button ever said anything about Dad. I think it's something he may have fantasized about, the way he decided certain skating judges conspired to keep him out of international competition.

Torvill insists on three pieces of toast, while Dean only eats things that are grape. All they want to talk about is their fifth birthday party, which is still an entire month away. It's right at the end of Rodeo Days, and Dean wants to have the party at the rodeo, with both a magician and a bucking bronco ride; Torvill wants to have a clown, pony rides, and a pizza party at Smiley's Pizza. They won't stop arguing, but at least Dean isn't kicking anything.

Dorothy sits quietly, ignoring them, and makes a giant stack of Cheerios that could win a record for tallest cereal tower ever. She eats the Cheerios that don't make it onto the tower.

The pears will have to wait.

I'd rather take the kids to IHOP, but I tried that once, a few months ago; it not only didn't work, it was the most stressful forty-five minutes of my entire life, especially when the roving balloon artist was making a rabbit and Dean reached up and popped the balloon with his fork.

Fortunately, Steve wasn't there to observe my hair with blueberry syrup and bacon toppings.

Steve. IHOP. Suddenly I remember what I've been trying to forget: Steve and that hostess. I push the thought away again. I can't think about that now. I'm pretending it didn't happen.

I toast myself a bagel, sit down at the table with the kids, and take the rubber band off the *Lindville Gazette*. Every article on the front page somehow relates to the upcoming Rodeo Roundup Days. The only front-page story *not* about the rodeo is about a gas-station robbery.

I don't want my parents reading that. They'll make me quit my job, and then I'll have no way of leaving the house, no way of repaying them, and I'll end up trapped here forever. I fold that section over and toss it into the recycle bin.

I open the next section. It's sports and obituaries. Softball games people have won, and cancer battles they have lost. In between are scattered giant ads for cars and trucks and, of course, Rodeo Roundup Days tickets.

"Come on, guys—it's almost time," I say, at 7:25.

Torvill hits the mute button on the TV and I flip on the radio perched on top of the refrigerator. It's preset to

1230 AM, KLDV, which has "traffic and weather on the nines." This is sort of absurd, because there isn't that much traffic here, and the weather does not change often. But KLDV has to do it, because the station is part of some big conglomerate radio network and that's one of their trademarks.

There's a little jingle, a very boppy and upbeat song that Dad helped to write, introducing KLDV's "Link to Mother Nature." It has this line that seems really dumb to me: "She has her ear to the ground, and her eye on the sky!" I always picture Mom lying on dew-covered grass with her head pressed against it, her clothes getting soaked as she gazes up at the sky, squinting because the sun is in her eyes.

She's live in the studio on weekday mornings, and then they tape her forecast and play it throughout the day until the night guy comes in. She occasionally does remotes, too. Sometimes I'll catch my mom describing what it's like outside by using her hands and making big, sweeping motions—the way she used to when she was a TV meteorologist.

"Good morning, KLDV listeners, and a special good morning to Dorothy, Torvill, and Dean," my mother says quickly, in her ultra-smooth radio voice, which is slightly perkier and also slightly huskier than her normal one—a weird combination that works.

"Mom, Mom, Mom!" Torvill screams.

"Shush," Dean tells her.

Dorothy dismantles her Cheerio tower and starts forming a cereal circle. "Sunny," she declares, announcing her own forecast. "Mostly sunny."

Mom only went back to work after the station told her she could say hi to her kids on at least *one* of the nines. They finally settled on 7:29, so every weekday morning I'm home with them I have to make sure we tune in. I told my mother not to say my name anymore, because it was embarrassing, but it feels kind of strange not to be on the list, like I'm not part of the family anymore.

"This is Christie Farrell, your link to Mother Nature, and here's today's weather outlook! Your morning temperature is sixty-eight degrees, up from an overnight low of sixty-two. But this coolness won't last long. We have an area of high pressure that's creating this gorgeous, hot sunny weather. Get ready for another scorcher. Today's high should be right around ninety. If you can find your way to a body of water—a pool, a lake, a river—jump in! If you're working outdoors, make sure you drink *plenty* of water to avoid dehydration. As always, there's a slight possibility of thunderstorms this afternoon, so keep an eye on the sky to be safe."

Everyone is so busy keeping an eye on the sky. Who's watching where they're going?

The telephone rings a minute later, so I go into my father's office to answer it. It's sort of like a skating museum, with bookshelves covered with pictures of Dad and trophies and medals he's won. There are a couple small trophies of mine on a top shelf, which I tried to convince Dad to put in the closet.

"Hello?" I say, grabbing the phone.

"Oh, hi, Peggy, it's Mom. I was just calling to make sure you were up."

"Mom, of course I'm up," I say. What's even worse than being expected to do so much is not being trusted to do it.

"Oh, good. Did you get a chance to tune in?"

"Of course we did," I say. "I never forget to do that."

"Well, did you eat the pears?"

"No, Mom," I say.

"Because they're ripe," she adds.

As she goes on and on about the fruit varieties in our crisper, I spin the globe next to my father's desk. I close my eyes and stick out my finger to stop the globe and see where I should head on my first worldwide trip.

"Peggy, are you listening?" Mom asks just as I open my eyes and see I've landed on Greenland.

"I'll check out the pears," I tell her as I spin the globe again.

Peggy, Peggy, Peggy

At 12:15 I am sitting on the front steps, watching the kids play, occasionally flipping through my French book, wondering how to say "Sorry I am so late" in French. Neither Mom nor Dad has called yet, and both are late. It has to be about ninety degrees outside. I take a deep breath and wish I hadn't. Today is definitely an 8 on the Lindville Aromatic Index: Stay inside and close the windows if you can. Light a candle.

I keep trying to convince the kids we should go inside where there's air-conditioning and better-smelling air, but they won't. Dean is practicing kickboxing against the garage door. Torvill is swinging on the swing set, and Dorothy is constructing castles in the sandbox that actually resemble European castles. Every time she finishes one, Dean comes over and kicks it down. Then Dorothy quietly, solidly, patiently rebuilds. She doesn't even cry. She never cries.

My father honks the horn as he finally pulls into the driveway. He gets out of the car and is wearing shiny black nylon warm-ups that fit like tights, and a red T-shirt with a cutoff bottom and arms. He has red-white-and-blue sweatbands around his wrists and forehead. His dark brown hair is standing up, styled by sweat—where he still *has* hair, that is. He has clogs on his feet, and his warm-up pants are three inches too short.

He looks like a refugee from a Broadway dance production. The guy who probably didn't get a callback.

Torvill, Dean, and Dorothy run to Dad and cling to his legs. I stand up and grab my backpack.

"So how was your workout?" I ask. My dad, the three kids, and I are all piled into his car. He's dropping me off at school, since he got home too late for me to skate there or take the bus. He's driving really fast, but I decide not to mention this. Driving instruction from me doesn't go over well with my parents.

"It wasn't great," he says. "My triple Salchow still isn't there, and I was seriously traveling on my spins. I just could not focus today." He is gracefully turning the wheel with one hand while he sips from a giant commuter mug of hot green tea in the other. He does everything semi-gracefully. It's his gift.

Still, my father is the most macho male figure skater I've ever seen. He never wore sequins when he competed. He wore only black, white, and various shades of gray, and—when he wanted to make a statement—a hat or a cap, like the one he wore for his Mary Poppins program, when he skated to "Chim Chim Cher-ee." Even when he was in the ice show, which had a lot of very embarrassing costumes, he got to be the tough guy—he'd play a policeman, or a dinosaur, or the Beast.

I admire my father tremendously for his athletic ability. When I watch old tapes of him, I can't quite believe this is the same guy. He volunteers at the town rink all winter, coaching little kids, getting people to donate their old skates, and organizing mini-shows. I took lessons from him, too, of course. We used to spend *hours* together while he tried to make me into a great skater.

The plan was sort of working, until one junior regional competition where I missed all my jumps and was on my rear end more than my skates. I don't like to think about it much. All I know is that I grew three inches in one year and suddenly nothing worked anymore. My dad took me to a sports psychologist for weeks afterward to try to help me deal with my "mental block," but it didn't work. It was like I had taken over someone else's body when I turned twelve, and I didn't have instructions on how to use it.

Let's just say that I don't spin well anymore.

"What's new with you?" Dad asks.

"Summer school. French class. Lots of homework," I say. "Gas station job. All very exciting."

"Don't worry, P. F.," my dad says. He likes to call me P. F. because those are his initials, too. "Things will pick up." He glances over at me and smiles. "Why don't you come down to the rink with me tomorrow? I could use a tough critic."

"I'm a tough critic?" I ask.

"Brutal," he says. "Remember when you said my back flip was the generic version of Scott Hamilton's? How everything I did was pewter-medal quality? Or wait. It could have been aluminum quality."

"Sorry about that. I was just mad because I couldn't do anything right that day myself. Remember?"

"I remember," my father says. "But you know, it has been a while since you tried, and you have been in-line skating a lot, so it could be time for *your* comeback, too."

"Right. Right, Dad. Sure," I say. "Any second now it's *all* going to fall into place."

"Don't laugh—that's how it happens," he says, signaling a turn. "So when can you come to the rink with me?"

"I don't know. Maybe in a couple of days—I have to see what my work schedule is for next week."

"I think you're too busy this summer. You should be relaxing, hanging out," Dad says.

This from the man who told me I had to take the job at Gas 'n Git because I had to pay him and Mom back, who asked me to take over breakfast duty so he could go skate this morning, who is now speeding into the Edison

High parking lot to drop me off for French class and I have only *une minute* to spare.

"Well, whenever you can make it," Dad says, and smiles at me.

I lean over and kiss his cheek before I get out of the car. Even though my dad can be annoying, I think he's the one person on earth who still has faith in me—even after everything. "Bye, guys!" I say to my sibs. "See you this afternoon."

"Peggy, Peggy, Peggy!" Torvill chants.

My name does not sound better when it's chanted in threes.

I see Charlotte racing across the parking lot toward me. I stop and wait for her, figuring it's better to be late together. I'll make up a story about the bus breaking down or something. *L'autobus était très tard.* Hopefully, Monsieur LeFleur, or a reasonable facsimile, will be too busy teaching to notice my bad grammar.

FEN

I'm sitting on the roof of Mrs. Duncan's car and I don't see Steve anywhere. Charlotte's lying on the hood, staring up past the towering streetlights at the night sky.

Charlotte's mother lets her borrow the car one night a month, and tonight is her lucky night. Instead of driving somewhere, though, we're parked at the Lot, and we're studying French. Or we're supposed to be.

This already feels like a routine for us, even though I've only known Charlotte a couple of days. She's just so easy to talk to, and since her friend Ashley is gone for the summer, too, we've instantly become best friends.

I like the new routine, except for the Steve-not-showing-up part. He's usually here with Mike Kyle, but I haven't seen Mike's Camaro yet tonight. Mike is one of Steve's best friends, but I don't know him that well. I just know they do everything together, but for some reason he won't talk to me—I'm not worthy enough. I don't really care what he thinks, except that if I knew him it might make it easier for me to hang out with Steve.

I have to be home by 10:00, so I'm running out of time here.

I've been waiting for Steve to show up since 8:00. Not that I know he's coming, for sure, but everyone ends up here on weekend nights whether they want to or not. I'm wondering if the IHOP girl was just a temporary fling, the way I guess *I* was. Maybe they only kiss at work. Maybe it's the allure of the blue vinyl booth. In any case, if Steve shows up by himself, I'm going to talk to him. It's been decided. By Charlotte.

I'm not sure how this particular parking lot ended up being the Lot. I guess in part because, since Discount Mania closed, the warehouse-size building has been vacant and there are no merchants to complain about us.

Another reason is that the Lot's a good turnaround spot for when people are cruising on Twelfth Street. The Lindville police have tried everything to stop the cruising on weekends, but nothing works. Every once in a while we all just have to drive up and down the same ten blocks, sitting and standing in the backs of pickups, or standing with our heads out of sunroofs, screaming at the top of our lungs. Usually it's a sporting event kind of thing—we won, or we might win, or we should have won—but sometimes it just comes out of nowhere, this accumulation of a need to scream. Maybe because we're stuck in

Lindville and we can't get out.

Charlotte's wearing a pair of faded jeans and a tiny pink T-shirt that says Brooklyn on it. Her hair fans over the car's hood and drifts in the breeze. "We have to be the only people here tonight even thinking of studying. Who studies in June? And on Friday night? Nobody."

"You're right," I say.

"So is he here yet?" she asks.

"No," I say. "You know what? Maybe we should quit talking about my love life and talk about yours instead."

"Well, back in Springfield I was seeing this guy Austin kind of seriously. But then we moved," Charlotte says. "He wanted to do the long-distance thing, but I said no way. So I thought I'd wait a little while and see if anyone here was worth going through all that again. Seriously depressing."

"And? Anyone yet?" I ask.

"Yeah. There's this guy at Shady Prairies."

"Isn't he a little *old* for you?" I ask.

"No!" Charlotte shrieks, and we both start laughing really hard. "He's not a resident. He *works* there," she says. "His name's Ray—he's seventeen. We hang out after work sometimes. He's got really nice arms."

"Arms." I nod. "Well, okay."

"Hey, you go crazy over a guy who makes pancakes, so I don't want to hear about it," Charlotte says.

"He doesn't *make* pancakes. He *serves* pancakes," I

correct her, and we laugh. "And he has nice arms, too."

"Yeah. So he's not here yet?" Charlotte asks again.

I survey the Lot. "Nope."

"He must have gotten stuck at work. Like in some syrup," Charlotte jokes. She sits up and steadies herself by grabbing the driver's-side mirror. Then she hops off the hood and straightens her T-shirt. "So should we walk around?"

"Definitely," I say as I scoot to the edge. My short denim shorts nearly get caught on the radio antenna as I slide to the ground. I don't know why I'm wearing shorts, because it really cools down at night here and I'm starting to shiver. Walking beside Charlotte, who's about four or five inches shorter than me, I feel very conspicuous. Suzanne is slightly taller than me—she plays volleyball and basketball—and I'm more used to walking around with someone my height.

"I doubt there's anyone here we even want to see," Charlotte says, "you know? I mean, who is even here?"

"I don't know," I say. It's different in the summer, because some people are away for the season; some are home. The thing we all have in common is that almost everyone seems bored.

Some people are running around, playing with a glow-in-the-dark Frisbee. Some are playing music out of their cars. Some people are smoking and some people are dancing and some are drinking.

"There's a FEN," I say as we check out a guy sitting on the tailgate of his pickup.

"A what?" Charlotte asks.

I laugh. "Sorry. FEN is the code word Suzanne and I came up with for new good-looking guys we haven't seen before. It stands for 'Further Evaluation Necessary.' We need to know more about them before we can proceed," I explain.

"FEN. I like it. Well, don't worry. We'll find out about him. We'll definitely evaluate as necessary," Charlotte says. "You know . . . maybe a physical evaluation."

We laugh, and while Charlotte stops to talk to a friend, I suddenly see Mike Kyle's Camaro, and Mike getting out and leaning against it. I walk toward him. Would it be rude for me to ask him to step aside so I can see if Steve's in the car?

Mike stares at me for a second.

"Hi," I say, feeling stupid because I'm by myself, and no one walks around the Lot by themselves. Also, Mike and I have talked all of three times before, and that was only because he was forced to acknowledge me because Steve was talking to me.

"Hey," he says. "What's up?"

"Not much. Really." I peer past him, wondering if Steve's back there somewhere in the clump of people getting out on the other side of the car.

"You're here this summer?" he asks with sort of a nice smile.

It seems sort of obvious, but I nod. "Yeah."

"I thought you went to camp," he says.

"Me? No. That was Suzanne," I say. Are we that interchangeable?

"Oh."

He's a sparkling conversationalist. But he looks good in a black T-shirt. That is something.

"Hey, Fleming," a girl with short black hair says, coming over to us. She was in my Current Events class last year, but I can't remember her name. "Savior" seems like a good name right now. She has about seven small earrings in one ear and one giant earring that looks like a metal bolt in the other.

"Hey," I say, smiling. I step away from Mike and closer to her. "How are you? How's your summer going?"

"It sucks," she says, as she peels a layer of polish off her thumbnail. "I'm working at my mom's salon. I sweep up hair."

"Well, I pour coffee at the Gas 'n Git," I say.

"Dead, disgusting hair," she says. "Sometimes dandruff."

"Okay, you win," I say, laughing.

A guy near Mike moves, and I notice Steve and the IHOP girl, Jacqui, leaning against the back of the car. They're standing so close that I can't even see air space between them. And they're kissing. Suddenly my good mood vanishes.

"So, Fleming, if you want to come by the salon, I can give you a free cut maybe—I'm learning," the girl says.

"Hey, uh, thanks," I mutter. "And if you ever want free coffee—you know where to find me." I quickly run off and find Charlotte and tell her we'd better get going or I'll miss my curfew.

"You look weird, Fleming. Your eyes are too bright or something. What just happened?" she asks.

"There's Steve—and that IHOP hostess again," I say, discreetly pointing in their direction. "And for some reason they have to kiss repeatedly in public."

Charlotte narrows her eyes at them. "Pig. But don't worry, you'll get him back."

"I can't get him *back*," I say.

"What are you talking about?" Charlotte says. "God, you're a hundred times prettier than she is."

I blush, hoping that's somehow true. "No. I mean, I can't get him back because I never had him in the first place," I admit. It was one thing when he wasn't seeing me, but he wasn't seeing anyone else, either. Then I could come up with theories about how he was a free spirit. Now he's happily chained to someone else.

"Oh. Well, that sucks." Charlotte pops her gum. "Forget him, okay? We've got FENs all over the place here."

"We've only seen one," I point out.

"Come on! Where there's one, there's more," Charlotte says. She puts her arm around my shoulders. "Let's get out of here. We're done studying. Right?"

"Considering that we never really started? Yeah," I say with a smile.

"We can do it on Sunday," Charlotte declares. "It's not like we have anything else to do on Sunday."

I think I'm supposed to go to a childbirth class with my pregnant mother on Sunday. Case in point.

"Anyway, if I don't get the car back on time, my mom won't let me have it next month," Charlotte says as we amble back toward her car.

As we start to pull out of the Lot, Mike and Steve come up beside us and pass us, peeling out onto Twelfth with squealing tires. I can't see if that Jacqui girl is with them. Maybe they ditched her, I think hopefully. Maybe Steve's realized that she's plastic, that he's made a terrible, horrible mistake. I can dream, for at least the next few seconds anyway, until we catch up to them at the next stoplight and I see her blond head in the rear window.

Your Love Is Like Roadkill

Saturday morning, Dad is busy getting three For Sale homes ready for their open houses—which means he makes sure the places have been vacuumed and de-cluttered, and he buys large floral arrangements. Dad's into flowers. I think he misses having them thrown onto the ice for him.

Mom has to do a radio remote from Gabe's Auto World. "I promise, Peggy, this is the *last* one," she said last night, which is what she said after the previous one. "I keep telling Bill, but he keeps saying they can't get by without me." And they can't, because Mom is great at remotes where she has to pitch products and run contests and interview shoppers. She has this gift. She can talk to anyone and never has dead air time.

I take Dorothy, Torvill, and Dean to the neighborhood playground, two blocks away. Because I'm the tallest person there, I end up holding all the neighborhood kids up to the overhead bar, which has a pulley that lets them slide to the other end. The kids scream my name and climb on me. They call me "Peggy the Gentle Giant." They don't get tired of doing this, but my arms get tired after fifteen minutes. Mrs. Klipp, from across the street, comes over to ask me how my summer's going, as if it's not obvious.

Mom gets home before Dad. She comes into the house, gets the kids started on lunch, and then turns to me. "So you're going to be here tonight, right?"

I'm in the middle of eating a banana so I have to swallow before I can ask, "Um, what?"

"You're going to be home tonight—to watch the kids?" she asks.

"Excuse me?" I say. "I am?"

"We're having dinner out with Laurie and Brandon, remember?" she says.

I shake my head.

"I left you a note," she says. She rifles through a stack of library books on the counter and a small piece of pink paper flutters to the floor. "Didn't you see this?" she asks as she struggles to bend down and pick it up.

"No," I say. "Nobody could have seen that."

"Oh, well." Mom hauls herself back up by the oven door handle. "We wanted to go out tonight, and I just thought—well, I didn't think you had any plans. So I figured you could watch the kids while we're out. We might be home kind of late—around midnight."

I can't say anything because I'm actually sort of stunned. Let me get this straight: I was here all morning watching the kids, and now they want me to be here all night, too? What if I had plans? What if I wanted to go out on Saturday night like most normal sixteen-year-olds?

I want to tell her that I can't, that I have plans, that it's going to be absolutely impossible. But it isn't. And besides, Mom has dark circles under her eyes where her makeup has sort of caked, and she looks exhausted. I'm not sure how going out with friends will help, but maybe it's what she needs. "I guess I could do it," I say.

"I knew you could! Did you hear that, guys? Peggy's going to hang out with you tonight," Mom says as she doles out sugar cookies. She doesn't even say "thanks" or "that's nice." She just says, "How about renting a movie?"

"Little Mermaid! Little Mermaid!" Torvill says.

"We don't have to rent that; we own it," Mom says, interrupting her before the third "Little Mermaid."

Do we ever, I think as I head up to my room, close the door behind me, and savor my few minutes of solitude. I turn up the radio and lie down on my bed, completely exhausted. I stare at the giant poster of New York City beside my bed, which is next to the poster of Boston, which is next to San Francisco. The other side of my room has framed prints of Provence, Rome, and London. The ceiling is a world map covered with neon-bright stickers to mark the places I want to go. Occasionally the stickers dry out and fall on me when I'm asleep and I wake up with DEFINITELY! or DUBLIN on my face.

I close my eyes and try to picture that it's a Saturday somewhere else. I'm shopping on Fifth Avenue. I'm standing by the ocean—no, I'm surfing in it. I have tickets for the ballet. I'm visiting ancient ruins or Buckingham Palace.

I'm not staying home in Lindville watching kids' videos I've seen a hundred times before.

Around three o'clock I skate to Gas 'n Git.

Denny is there, writing in his notebook between gas transactions, and wants to know what I'm doing. "You're here on your day off. *Why?*" He puts down his pen and looks up from his notebook.

"To pick up my check. And I'm getting presents for a friend." I want to send Suzanne a care package.

"You mean *gitting*, don't you?" Denny asks. "Please use the trademarked phrase while in the store. Jamie's here today, you know—better not do anything un-employee-like."

I shrug. "Okay. So how's it going?"

"Everyone's grumpy because the pay-at-the-pump receipt printers aren't working, and apparently it's a tragedy." Denny rolls his eyes.

"Devastating," I agree.

"Jamie's trying to fix them. She's on the phone with

Gas 'n Git Central. In the meantime, no one has to prepay, but everyone still comes in here in a bad mood," Denny says. There's a little crackle on his gas-pump monitor, and Denny clicks the speaker and says, "You're okay on seven . . . Kevin." He looks out the front window and waves at a guy who's filling up. "See, I know him, and that rhymes, so it's sort of cool."

"Sort of," I say.

"Hey—while you're here, you mind listening to some lyrics? I'm sort of stuck," Denny admits.

"Um. Okay," I say. I can see how he would be stuck, if *seven* and *Kevin* are what he's working with. I'm actually very curious to hear what Denny writes about. His motorcycle, I'm guessing—and his accessories. Or about the cruelty of wanting a mustache and not being able to grow one.

Denny clears his throat. "This town has no soul, it's a hollow shell with nothing to fill it," he begins to sing. It sounds suspiciously like a familiar U2 song, but with different lyrics. "But with you by my side—no, wait, that wasn't it." He peers at the words on the page. "But you won't give in. You won't give in. And your life has gone . . ."

"Country?" I say.

He frowns at me. "No. Your life has gone—"

"To the dogs," I suggest.

"Shut up," he says. "Your life has gone around the bend, and your love is like a . . . well, I wanted to put in

64

something about the road. Your love is like a stop sign?" he asks.

"Speed bump," I suggest. "Or how about roadkill? Your love is like roadkill."

"You're really awful at this," Denny says. "Come on, just actually try to help me, okay? How about . . . Your love makes me yield. I can't yield to your love. No—I can't *stop* for your love."

"But you can at least slow down and let me jump out of the car," I say. "Right?"

Denny frowns at me.

"What—I was serious," I say, thinking of Kamikaze Bus Driver, how this song could be his theme.

"Okay, then. Next song." Denny tears the sheet of paper out and crumples it into a ball and then flips to a fresh page in his notebook.

"Your love is a crumpled page," I say.

Denny taps his pen against the counter. Then he looks at me. "That's not bad."

"And I can't throw it away," I add.

"Okay, *that* is bad."

"Fleming!" Jamie says. Our boss walks out of the back office and dumps a stack of receipt-paper rolls on the counter. "How are you? What a coincidence that you dropped by. I need to talk to you."

"Coincidence?" Denny scoffs. "Not exactly. Our pay-checks are ready."

Me, I'm worried that she needs to talk to me. She's not going to fire me. Is she?

"I have a problem, and I was wondering if you could help out," Jamie goes on. "I've lost my Saturday-night coffee person."

"Thank *God*," Denny says as he swipes a customer's credit card. "That guy was—"

Jamie clears her throat loudly and we move away from the counter a bit. "Anyway, I was wondering if it would be at all possible for you to pick up the shift."

"You mean . . . permanently?" I ask. Can my summer get worse? I have to work on Saturday nights now?

"Yes. We could trade it for your Friday day shift, because I have someone who can cover that," Jamie says. "So what do you think? The shift is from three to eleven, and you'd be working with Denny."

I stare at the freezer and contemplate my options. Working with Denny isn't bad, because he's a known quantity. And I can either work here or risk being stuck at home. And I know that Steve has worked Saturday nights forever, so I wouldn't be missing anything there. And I do have to keep this job. "I'll do it, but I can't start tonight," I say.

"That's fine. That's perfect. You're a *life*saver," Jamie tells me. Then she goes over to replenish the coffee tanks.

I wander around, shopping, while Denny rings up gas sales. As soon as Jamie goes back to the office, Denny rushes over and shuts off the coffee machines. He dumps more coffee into the filters, then presses the "Resume" buttons.

"What are you doing?" I ask.

"She makes the worst coffee. God. Undrinkable. She doesn't use enough, and it comes out tasting like dirty water," Denny says.

"So why do we sell Jamie's Java Blend?" I ask. "And why is she here making coffee when she doesn't usually?"

"Rick didn't show up for like the hundredth time, so she fired him. So, you taking the Saturday-night shift?"

"Yeah," I say.

"Cool. So you're here to buy stuff. Why aren't you shopping at the mall?" he asks.

"Employee discount. Plus, it's too far away," I say. "Plus, there aren't any good stores there."

"True. Very true. I *long* for a decent store in this town," Denny says.

"You could write a song about that," I say.

Denny smiles. "Right." He comes out from behind the counter and follows me around the store.

There are only three aisles of food and auto supplies. I grab a rain bonnet and two packets of ibuprofen. I get a plastic coffee mug with the Espress-Oh-Yes logo for Suzanne, and then head for the candy aisle. I stack chocolate bars and bags of fruit-flavored candies in my arms.

"So what is all this for?" Denny asks.

"It's a care package," I tell him. "My friend's a camp counselor, and you know how camp food sucks."

Denny shakes his head. "Not really. I've never gone to camp. I'm not exactly a camp-type person."

"What kind of person is that?" I ask.

"You know. The kind of person who likes living in a cabin with a bunch of other people and hiking and sitting around a campfire. Roasting marshmallows. Singing. All together." Denny shudders.

"You sing," I say. "You like singing. You write songs."

"They do *skits*, okay? I don't think I need to say any more." Denny rushes over to ring up another gas sale.

A few minutes later I carry my stash of gifts to the counter and drop them in front of him. "Ring away."

He starts scanning the items and asks, "What are you doing tonight?"

I really hope he isn't trying to ask me out. I know he isn't—that he wouldn't. But the question always makes me think that, anyway. "Hanging out with my sibs," I say. "Technically you could call it baby-sitting, except I'm their big sister."

"Baby-sitting. On Saturday night," Denny says.

"Yes."

"You are *exciting*," he says. "Do you know that?"

He's acting like this was *my* idea. "At least I won't be working *here*. Yet."

"And at least I'm not at camp. Give your friend my

sympathy, okay? Here." He grabs a few packs of spearmint gum, pays for them, and tosses them into the plastic bag. "She'll need these. They don't let you brush your teeth much when you're at camp. You have to go down to the river or whatever."

"Thanks," I say, surprised by his generosity.

"No problem. Rvoyr," Denny says.

I stare at him for a second until I realize what he's saying. "Yeah. *Au revoir* to you, too."

On my way home, an eighteen-wheeler veers into the bike lane and nearly dusts me.

This town has no soul. And nobody yields to your love. Nobody yields, period.

Maternity Moments

I am sitting on the floor of the Lindville Medical Center's Lamaze Lounge. I am the only female in the room with a flat stomach. My mother is fifteen minutes late for our first childbirth class. The other people sitting in our circle are mothers, and fathers, and unborn babies. People are looking at me and wondering why I'm not "showing" yet, why I don't *have* a partner, why I'm in this class when I am so obviously not pregnant. "People!" I want to say. "It's not me!" I cannot believe Mom isn't here yet. I can't believe she's doing this to me. This is so embarrassing.

I'm only here because Mom wants us to "bond" by having me there for her next—and she claims her last—baby delivery. I don't know how I feel about it. Most of the time I'm either scared or disgusted, but every now and then I'm sort of flattered. Only . . . what if the next baby comes out kicking like Dean?

The Lamaze Lounge is on the fifth floor of the hospital,

just past the nursery. I'd think just being here for the first time could make you need some deep-breathing techniques. Just to walk past the maternity ward and hear some of the screams coming out of those rooms. What really gets to me about being in hospitals is the smell, a disgusting mixture of chemical cleansers, disinfectants, hot cafeteria food . . . and things you don't want to think about.

If Mom doesn't show up, maybe I'll check into the ear, nose, and throat ward, see what they can do about my heightened sense of smell. Maybe they could use plastic surgery to rebuild my nose, take out all the sensors while simultaneously making it perfect and cute, like plastic hostess-girl Jacqui's.

I've never been to the hospital for myself, but I've been here on the fifth floor twice before. Torvill and Dean took a while to arrive, so Dad and I camped out here together in uncomfortable orange chairs. Dorothy was born more quickly, and I stayed home with the twins and my grandparents.

We're in this class basically for me. Mom knows everything already. She knows the doctors, the nurses, the procedures, the gift-shop hours, and even the best vending machines.

"Peggy! I thought we were meeting at home," Mom says as she rushes into the lounge. She looks like she just got off a bike. She's wearing black Lycra shorts, a yellow jersey, and her hair is wet with sweat. She looks like she is fresh off the Tour de Lindville.

"Mom, you left me a note telling me to meet you here," I say. I look around at everyone in the room. See? I want to say to the rest of the class. It's *her* we're here for. Not me. You can save your lectures on teen sex. Believe me. I have nothing going on, so they'd be wasted on me.

"I did? Really? Wow. Is it me, or am I going straight from having babies to having memory loss? It's like one minute you're having maternity moments . . . you know, where you can't get out of a chair . . . to senior moments, where you can't remember where the chair *is*." She sits down carefully on the carpeted floor, her round belly stretching the yellow nylon top, her belly button showing through the fabric.

She's just so clueless when it comes to maternity clothes that it's almost cute. Almost. She just starts wearing Dad's clothes and lots of XLs. When she was pregnant with Torvill and Dean, she bought some XXLs. Friends always try to give her their old maternity clothes, but she won't take them, unless they're maternity sportswear.

My mother is a very good athlete, which is probably why she can handle her pregnancies so well. She's really into cycling, but she kind of takes the bike shorts a little too far, in my opinion. Early in your ninth month, maybe you shouldn't be wearing maternity bike shorts, even if they make them.

"Welcome, class, welcome!" The teacher, Monica, is bright and sparkly and also pregnant, but not nearly as far along. "I'm so glad you're all here to begin this wonderful journey with me." She looks at me and smiles, with a semiconfused look on her face.

I want to tell her: Nobody could feel more confused about me being here than I am.

"As you probably know, this class will teach you various methods of preparing for the joyful experience of giving birth to your child," Monica continues. "You'll learn valuable relaxation and visualization techniques, do breathing exercises—and of course we'll practice some ways to make you more comfortable during your labor."

"Like anyone can be comfortable during labor," Mom says under her breath to me.

I start to giggle, and Monica suddenly fixes her gaze on us, like we're the problem students that need to be reined in early to set an example for the rest of the class. "So, why don't we start by introducing ourselves?" she says, her smile a little less wide. "Perhaps *you* could start." She gestures to Mom.

"I'd be glad to," Mom says in her super-cool radio voice. "I'm Christie Farrell, and—"

"Christie Farrell—from KLDV?" a woman across the room asks eagerly. My mother nods. "Oh, my gosh, I listen to your forecasts *every* morning."

"Well, thank you very much," my mother says with a polite smile.

"You're usually right. Except about that snowstorm back in March," the woman says.

"Yes. Well, the moisture indicators simply weren't there, what can I tell you?" Mom's smile fades as the woman describes how she was stranded without a coat or a windbreaker and how awful it was. Mom hates having her forecasts criticized. She's a perfectionist, like Dad— she'd do her forecasts over if she could. She has this framed Mark Twain quote over her desk: "Everybody talks about the weather, but nobody does anything about it." Then she has a neon-pink Post-It stuck onto the glass that says, "But I'll keep trying."

Monica clears her throat and says, "I'm sorry, could we get back to the introductions? Please?" She holds out her hand toward my mother. "Christie, if you could continue?"

"Yes. Well, this is Peggy," my mother says, still disregarding that I'd rather be called Fleming. "She's going to be my birth coach this time. I thought it would be fun for us to do this together. I've been here before, of course, but this is all new to Peggy."

Monica studies us for a second. "You know, I'm so glad you're here. This can be a *very* bonding experience for a stepmother and daughter."

"Yes, well, I'm her mother. Not her stepmother." Mom smiles awkwardly. "Just to sort of clarify. I know we don't look much alike right now, but that's because I've got this baby here and I haven't been able to get my hair highlighted. But you can see she got my height, and we've both got lots of freckles. You see, what happened was, my husband and I had Peggy when we were quite young, and so then we decided to wait a while before we had more children. So we waited, and now we have three little ones at home, and we've definitely got our work cut out for us with another baby coming, don't we, Peggy?"

Work cut out for me, *you mean*, I'm thinking. They love Mom at KLDV, because she can talk and talk and talk and easily fill dead air and easily fill in for sick DJs and easily do a remote from a car dealer or a new store or even the rodeo. But when I'm with her? I wish she wouldn't.

"Before we start today, can I ask anyone else if they get really bothered by all this high pressure?" Mom goes on. "I feel like it's so dry that my body on purpose starts retaining more water than it needs to. I mean, I could just use a nice, heavy rain for a couple of days."

Oh, my God. I'm dying here. Why does she have to do this? Why does she have to talk about water retention and weather? I ignore her voice and count to ten. When I stop counting, she's still talking.

"Excuse me, Christie? We'd better get going with the rest of our introductions," Monica says, still smiling. She moves on to the next couple, who can barely talk. They're just staring at us like we rolled in from a traveling carnival, like we're in the Rodeo Roundup Days Stranger than Fiction stage show.

Mom reaches over and squeezes my knee. "You look sick. Are you feeling all right?" she asks softly. "It's so hot in here, isn't it? I feel a little faint myself." She leans back against me and stretches out her legs.

Deep breathing techniques can't come soon enough for both of us.

Everyone Looked Dead

"Hey, it's Tonya Harding. What's up?" Denny is in a cheery mood when I show up for work on Monday at 5:45 A.M.

I glare at him. I can't believe he's calling me "Tonya." I've just been almost chomped on by the Doberman, who got so close that his slobber rained on my leg when he barked at me. I grab my checkered apron from the closet in back and put it on over my red-striped T-shirt and black capris. Not a good outfit, because the apron is so long I look like I'm not wearing pants, but I was too sleepy to think about it when I got dressed at 5:00. I go behind the counter and start prepping the machines, brewing coffee, organizing sweetener packets, restocking the cups, filling the Thermos containers with milk and half-and-half.

"Hey," Denny says when there's a break in the action. "Did you hear what happened at the Conoco on Twelfth yesterday?"

"No, what?" I ask.

"They got held up last night," Denny says. "It was even on TV because I guess that's the fourth robbery around here in the last two weeks. They had a reporter there and everything. The lighting is really terrible at that Conoco. Everyone looked dead. I mean, if we get robbed, we've got to think about where we should stand when they interview us."

I'm not thinking about being photogenic. I'm still stuck on the words *dead* and *robbery*. "Did anything bad happen?" I ask. "Did anyone get hurt?"

"Nah. They hadn't safed the money yet, so they lost several hundred bucks. But don't worry," Denny says. "I got the guy's description. They said he's between five-six and six feet tall, and he wears sunglasses and a baseball cap as a disguise."

"*That* really narrows it down," I say.

"Hey—it's something to go on," Denny says. "Also, he has brown hair and a mustache."

"Again. We're talking about half the population of Lindville," I say. The other half either don't want a mustache, or includes guys, like Denny, who obviously want one but can't grow one. His has gone from lint to fuzz, but seems to have paused there.

Denny shrugs. "The guy supposedly has this fixation with scratch tickets. At least that's what he pretends to buy. Then, while the clerk reaches down to tear them off for him, the guy pulls out a handgun and asks for all the cash in the register."

"A *gun*? Really?" I don't want to imagine a thief walking in here. I decide that I'm never filling in for anyone on the gas side of Gas 'n Git. I'll only serve coffee. I won't go near scratch tickets. "So, do you think he'll ever come here?" I ask nervously.

"One can only hope," Denny says.

"Hope?"

"Don't you want to be on TV?" Denny asks.

"That depends. Will I be alive or dead?" I ask.

Then again, I have such bad luck that I probably work at the only place that won't be robbed. Nothing that exciting will ever happen here.

About five minutes later, a guy in a baseball cap and sunglasses comes in and tells Denny he wants one "Six-Bun Salute" ticket and one "Prospector's Gold Nugget." Denny looks over at me and grins before reaching under the glass to get the tickets.

He's the kind of person who really would enjoy being robbed. He could set the scene to music, something by U2, of course.

The customer asks for cigarettes, pays, and leaves.

"Yeah, well. Maybe next time," Denny says with a loud sigh.

I feel sort of fidgety and start restocking the mint and candy dish. Then I take paper cups and fill them with mints, too, and stagger them along the counter so there's no way people can miss them. World's Worst Coffee Breath is on his way, and I will get to him sooner or later.

I don't know how this wall of mints will save me from a man with a handgun, though. I'll pretend it's a fort, and duck.

I feel very stupid as I get onto the Lindvillager at noon and hand Kamikaze Driver his cup of coffee. I hold the cup out to him and feel everyone on the bus staring at me, maybe a little jealously. This could establish a dangerous precedent. Soon I'll be carrying trays of coffee to the bus. I'll be the world's first bus attendant.

"You didn't say whether you wanted cream and sugar." I give Kamikaze a handful of sugar, sweetener, and nondairy creamer packets, which he stuffs into various compartments and cup holders in the dashboard.

"Cream, next time. The real stuff," he grumbles.

"Okay, but I don't take the bus every day," I say. "Usually Mondays, Wednesdays, and Thursdays, but—"

"I know your schedule," he says.

The way he says it makes me think of a TV movie. *He Knew Her Schedule: The Peggy Fleming Farrell Story*. Since when is a bus driver keeping tabs on me? And why? Just because he needs coffee? So why not bring a Thermos in the morning, like a normal person?

Then for some reason he keeps looking at me, not

closing the door. He's waiting for something. "Fare, please," he says.

I drop my quarters into the box.

Then he holds out his hand.

"I just paid," I say. "See the green light?"

"Change, please," he insists.

I sigh and take out some change from my pocket. I can't believe he wants change back from his coffee purchase. I delivered it onto a *bus*. This guy has no idea what I went through, carrying a hot paper cup up a steep slope.

I am about to say something when he shuffles the money around in his hand and then gives me back a quarter. "Thank you," he says. "Next time there will be more in it for you."

"I'm so grateful," I say.

Kamikaze sips his coffee, then charges back into traffic before I can even take a seat. I reach out for a seat back to hold on to, but the bus swerves and I fall onto the end of a seat that's already taken, right into the lap of none other than Mike Kyle.

I'm shocked. Mike's never been on this bus before. This runs against the laws of nature. I'm just so stunned that I can't help blurting, "What are you doing here?" completely impolitely. Then I realize I'm still sitting on his lap. There's a really awkward moment where I have to untangle my bag from where it's wrapped around Mike's knee. "I mean, *sorry*," I say as I get up and move to the seat behind him.

"No problem, don't worry about it," Mike says. He sort of smiles. His face has that lean and chiseled look, like he could pose for something, but I'm not sure what. Maybe a calendar of hot high-school guys who don't go to class all that often.

"Sorry," I say again, putting my bag on the floor in front of me. "It's just . . . his driving. It's hard to stay uninjured."

"Yeah. So what was that? You brought him coffee? Like, personal delivery?" Mike asks. "Is he your dad or something?"

"No!" I say firmly. "We're not related. He asked me to do it, and I have to take this bus three days a week, so . . ."

"He's kind of scary, so you do it. I get it. You know, he almost just took out a guy on a moped back there." Mike gestures to the back window.

"You're kidding," I say. "No one rides mopeds here. That's like something out of my French book."

"Your what book?"

"French? Summer school?" I shake my head. "Never mind."

"Yeah, okay." He turns back around and looks out the window for a minute.

I stare at the back of his head, at his dark brown hair. He's good-looking, but in an unconventional way. I never really noticed before, because when he's around, Steve's around.

Mike turns back to me and asks, "So what are you doing this summer? I thought you went to work at some camp."

"No, that was my friend Suzanne," I tell him. Again. "I'm working at Gas 'n Git, and, well . . ." I decide not to go into the birth-coaching, debt-paying, baby-sitting glamour of it all. "That's pretty much it."

"Oh. Well, that's cool."

This is bizarre. Mike Kyle is actually making conversation with me. He's barely ever acknowledged my existence before. He always sort of looked at me vacantly, as if either he or I weren't there. Is it because we're both stuck on a bus with a crazy driver? People definitely bonded in that *Speed* movie.

I think maybe I should keep the conversation going. If I can talk to Mike, maybe I can get closer to Steve. This has never been my m.o., but obviously my previous M.O. wasn't working all that well and I clearly need to make adjustments.

Kamikaze honks the horn at something, pulls over at another stop, and then spins the wheel. We're back in action, as another rider lurches into her seat.

"So. How come you're riding the bus?" I ask. "Is your Camaro in the shop?" I lean forward and rest my elbows on the back of his seat.

"Ha. Good one. My Camaro." His lips get this pinched, skin-too-tight look, like being alive and breathing suddenly hurts.

"Oh. Sorry," I say quietly.

"It was my dad's. He took it back. He got really mad at me because Gropher and I were racing it Saturday night, out in the fields."

"Saturday night? You mean . . . after I saw you?" I ask.

He nods. "Yeah. My dad said I didn't respect the car or something. Just because I ran over some cornstalks."

"Cornstalks?" I ask, my eyes widening. "What happened? How did he find out about it?"

"There was corn in the driveway. I mean, not actual *corn* corn, because it's too early for that, but there were stalks. He was furious. He cleaned out the car and he's selling it now. He gave me this lecture. It completely sucks. I can't do anything for the rest of the summer, basically." Mike rolls his eyes. "I have to take this bus or ride my bike everywhere. It's the pits."

"I know," I say. "I'm in the same boat. I mean, um, bus." I laugh nervously. There's a very awkward moment of silence, where I wait for him to say more, and wait for me to come up with something else to say. I decide to plunge right into what I really want to know. "So what are you and Steve going to do now?" I ask. Besides hang out with IHOP hostesses? "I mean, it's kind of a long summer if you don't have a car. Trust me."

"Yeah. I know. I guess I'll have to get a better job,"

Mike says. "Earn enough money to buy my own car."

"What about Steve? Why doesn't he buy a car?" I ask.

"I *know*." Mike slaps the seat back of the older passenger in front of him, startling him. "God, he makes me mad. He's holding on to all his money so he can buy a van or a truck next year and drive all over the country. Some stupid plan like that."

I smile. Some stupid plan that I want to be *in* on. Although the van concept is a little disturbing. I remember my aunt and uncle's conversion van, completely decked out with furniture and a fridge—and tacky decorations.

I tell myself to stop picturing a van with wall-to-ceiling leopard-print carpeting, and focus. I'll never be anywhere near that van unless I get close to Steve again. I have weird goals. I realize that. "So, um, what are you doing for work now?" I ask.

"Delivering the *Gazette*," Mike says. "On my bike."

"You?" I squeak, before I can stop myself.

"Yeah, me," he says. "Why is that so surprising?"

"You have to be up . . . really, really early," I say. "I always thought you were one of those, I don't know. Night owls. Staying up all night watching movies with Steve or whatever."

"I don't sleep much," Mike says. "I kind of don't like sleeping."

I stare at him. Who doesn't like sleeping?

"Whoa, here's my stop." He pulls the wire to let Kamikaze Driver know he should think about pausing. "See you around."

"See you," I say as I watch Mike stand by the steps, ready to get off the bus. He has no butt to speak of. He has bony hips and then his jeans just sort of free-float until they hit his red flip-flops.

"Back of the white line," Kamikaze grumbles at him loudly.

Mike turns to me and rolls his eyes. "Help me," he mouths.

And we exchange smiles.

Then the Lindvillager screeches to a stop at the corner of Twelfth and Arizona, Mike nearly falls down, and then gets off the bus, and we're back on the road in under five seconds.

I just had the longest conversation with Mike Kyle that I, or perhaps anybody, has ever had. I learned that he's an insomniac with a paper route and an urge to destroy crops. He's really not so bad.

Sunny-side Down

After French class on Wednesday, Charlotte and I go to IHOP, even though I tell her it's pointless, that Steve and Jacqui are an item now.

"It's not pointless," she says. "You give up way too easy, Fleming."

"I do?" I ask. Because I thought I actually held on way too long.

"Yes," she says. "Make the guy see what he's missing already. Besides, I'm hungry."

Before we go inside IHOP, Charlotte and I pause in the parking lot of the hardware store next door so I can brush my hair. Charlotte insists on quickly braiding it into a thick French braid that, from what I can see in the hardware-store window, looks pretty good. I'm wearing low-cut faded jeans and a mint-green cap-sleeved T-shirt which fortunately doesn't have any coffee stains, thanks to my lovely Gas 'n Git apron. Charlotte pulls a tube of essential oil out of her purse and I put a few drops on my neck.

"I feel so essential," I tell her.

"Good," she says.

When we get to IHOP, I'm thrilled to see that Jacqui isn't working. We get seated in Steve's section. Everything seems to be going my way.

Charlotte taps her menu against the table as she gazes at Steve, who's walking toward us. "I'll stall him here as long as I can, don't worry. *Not* a problem at all. I can talk forever if I have to."

Just like my mom, I think. I hold my breath as Steve comes up to our table and stops. I let it out halfway and say, "Hey."

"Hey, Fleming. What's up?" Steve smiles. "How's French?"

"Finegood," I say, momentarily flustered and unable to choose a word. "I mean, *très bien*."

"Yes. Of course that's what you mean," Steve says. "I knew right away."

I feel my face turning red, contrasting with the cool mint T-shirt color. I want to ask him why he didn't take the class, like he was supposed to, but for some reason it would seem like whining, so I don't. "So, this is Charlotte. She's new here."

"Hardly," Charlotte tells him. "I feel like I've been here forever."

"Yeah. That's what we call the Lindville Effect. Right,

Fleming?" Steve looks at me and smiles.

"Exactly," I say, feeling like the connection between us definitely isn't gone. It might be faint right now, like a bad cell phone connection, but it's still there.

"So, just to get the formalities out of the way, in case you guys are secret shoppers, taking notes on everything I do. My name is Steve and I'll be your server this afternoon."

I don't ever get tired of hearing him say that. I really don't.

"Did you get burned by a secret shopper recently or something?" I ask him.

"Oh, yeah. But I don't want to go into that right now." He glances over his shoulder toward the kitchen, as if he's being watched. I wonder if a secret shopper mentioned that he was too busy making out with a coworker to be a good server. Maybe he and Jacqui will be *forced* to break up. "So what can I get you?" he asks. "Or do you need a little more time with the menus?"

I need a little more time with the server, actually. But I don't want to be any more obvious than I'm already being. "I think I'm ready. Are you?" I ask Charlotte.

"I'm not sure. I was going to get French toast, you know, *vive la France* and all that. But now I'm thinking maybe just a two-egg combo thingy. Or three eggs. Yeah, that sounds good. Hey, go wild, make it a half dozen," she says.

"Are you serious?" Steve asks. He looks at Charlotte

as if she's crazy. "I don't think you can order that."

"Sure I can. The three-egg combo plate, with three eggs on the side," Charlotte says.

"Three eggs on the side?" Steve repeats.

She looks up at Steve and smiles. "No, I guess just the two-egg thingy. Please."

"How would you like those two eggs?" Steve asks.

"Well, that's another thing. I have some egg questions," Charlotte says.

Steve raises his eyebrows.

"What does it mean, exactly, when it's sunny-side up? Is there a sunny-side down?" Charlotte asks.

"No. See, there's the sun. Which faces up," Steve says. "And then when you flip the egg over, it's called over easy."

"Hmm. I'll have to think about that. You go ahead, Fleming. I'll be ready in a second," Charlotte says.

While I order, I admire Steve's blue apron. It's not something you notice when it's on anyone else. But it's got this way of bringing out Steve's eyes, sort of the way my checkered-flag apron brings out the dark circles under my eyes at 6 A.M.

After I order, he turns to Charlotte. "And for you?" he asks.

"I'm not quite ready yet," she says.

Steve stands there. He glances at the tables around us to check on his other customers. He looks at me and smiles awkwardly.

"So. French. How is it, being in school when it's a hundred degrees?" he asks.

"Fine. The teacher's never there. I mean, we have subs," I say. Today's substitute looked like she had just come from playing golf, and was more concerned with her score card than with whether or not we could make any sense of the learn-French-by-video we were watching. "Really bad subs," I say.

"Huh," Steve says.

"Really bad," I repeat.

Steve just nods.

And I can't think of anything else to say. I fidget with my braid. The conversation is dead in the water. I nudge Charlotte's foot with mine. I need help.

She looks up at me, and then clears her throat. "So I want two eggs, sunny-side down," she tells Steve. "And if the cook says there isn't such a thing, just explain that I like saying that better than *over easy*. Okay? And I want pancakes and bacon."

"Sounds good. I'll be right back," he says. Then he leaves for the kitchen.

I watch him walk away, thinking: How did I blow it? Again? Why can't I think of anything to say? Why couldn't I have just asked him about movies he's seen lately, or the Camaro-cornstalk incident, or mention I saw Mike on the bus? Why does my brain atrophy like that?

"You know how you could really make him notice you?" Charlotte asks.

I shake my head. "Obviously not."

"Dine and dash." She raises her eyebrows. "Take off when the check comes. He'd have to run after you and tackle you then. And once that happened, well, it's all up to you what happens next." She grins. "Am I right?"

"Are you serious?" I ask her.

"Yes!" she says happily.

It's not the worst plan I've heard of, I think. But it's close. "I'd only do it if I could be sure he'd be the one who chased me. If Roger, that other waiter, ended up tackling me? That would be gross."

"Yeah, he'd probably break his glasses. I guess the whole plan is a little stupid and desperate." Charlotte shrugs. "I wouldn't mind doing the dine and dash, though. It might be exciting, and as we both know, we could use a little more excitement around here. I mean, this summer is off to a really slow start."

I nod. "I have to agree."

"Do you ever feel like doing something totally crazy? Just to shake things up, just to get someone's attention?"

Like talking to Mike Kyle on the bus? "Whose attention do you want?" I ask Charlotte.

"I don't even know. Someone's. Anyone's," Charlotte says. "The whole town's, maybe. It's so boring, like everyone's asleep."

"It's the heat," I say. "Or maybe the bad air."

"It might be smelly, but it's not carbon monoxide," Charlotte says. "There's actually no excuse."

"You could do something during the Rodeo Days," I suggest. "Be in the parade. Wear a really outrageous costume."

Charlotte thinks about it for a few minutes, then says, "I know. How about if I *don't* wear a costume? How about if I streak naked down the street?" she asks, just as Steve comes up to the table with our platters of eggs and pancakes.

Steve obviously overhears, because his hand wobbles as he tries to put our plates down. The sunny-side-down eggs that Charlotte ordered slither off the plate onto the table, nearly skidding into my lap. One of the yolks breaks and spreads slightly, but it's stopped by a hardened ridge of syrup on the table that holds it in, like a dam. All that's between me and Steve now is an egg moat.

"Of course, you guys are going to streak with me," Charlotte says. "I'm not doing it by myself."

Steve quickly grabs a wet dishrag from a nearby service cart. As he cleans the eggs off the table, he looks up at me, with a little smile that verges on being flirtatious. "Well, uh, what do you say, Fleming? Are we in?" he asks. I think he's adventurous enough that he just might.

"That depends," I say, looking right at him, wanting him to know I am serious about being seriously interested

93

in him. As if he doesn't know that yet. "Can I wear my Rollerblades? Because I'd want to be moving pretty fast, I think, if I was streaking in a parade."

"You guys could both be on in-line skates. You could skate *together*. You know, like nude pairs skating, or whatever!" Charlotte says excitedly.

"Yeah, but, uh, I don't actually skate, and if I fell . . ." Steve blushes, as if he has just in fact imagined it, as if he's gotten a vivid mental picture of a naked me, on in-line skates, and a naked him. He picks up Charlotte's plate and drops the dirty dishrag onto it. "So I'll get you a new order of, uh, those eggs. Be right back." He shuffles off toward the kitchen, and Charlotte and I crack up laughing.

"I can't believe you said that to him!" I gasp between laughs. "God, that was so embarrassing."

"Hey, you're the one who brought up the Rollerblade part!" she shoots back.

"*Nude* pairs skating?" I can't stop laughing. "What is that?"

"Hey, you're the skater. You tell *me*," Charlotte says.

I sit back in the booth and smile. Steve might be seeing Jacqui, but for a second there he was thinking about streaking with me—and he didn't seem to mind.

Triple Ew

"**M**onsieur LeFleur is still under the weather," a new substitute informs us when we gather for our fifth French class.

Monsieur LeFleur must have something sort of serious, I think. He is supposed to be so dedicated to teaching that he broke up his marriage over doling out too much extra help on weekends. Well, that and the weeklong trips with the high-school French Club—which is 90 percent female—to Quebec every spring. If he can't drag himself out of bed for a simple summer session, then he must have a monster flu. Or something more serious.

It figures. Not only did Steve not take this class, now the teacher isn't even taking it.

"He doesn't have that flesh-eating bacteria, does he?" I ask today's substitute.

"What? No, of course not," the sub says. "What made you ask *that*?"

I shrug. "It seems like a thing that could make you miss a lot of classes, that's all."

"Yes. I mean, you might think he's seriously ill, but no, he's going to be fine," the sub says. "Just can't actually quite get out of bed yet. The vice principal told me he hasn't had a sick day in eight years, which sounds sort of sick in itself to me, know what I mean?" He smiles, and there's something green stuck between his front teeth. "But don't give up on him. Don't you *dare*. Not our Monsieur LeFleur."

"Okay. Sorry." I look over at Charlotte, and she shrugs.

"Now. He requested that we use today's class time to make a videotape," the substitute says. "He would like you all to introduce yourselves, so that when he returns, he'll already know you and you can jump right into the curriculum."

We go around the room, starting with me. I think the substitute is trying to give me extra attention because I seemed so distraught with my flesh-eating-disease comment.

"*Je m'appelle* . . . Fleming Farrell," I say, as quickly as I can, realizing that I've just made a horrible rhyme because I pronounced Farrell "Far-*elle*," as if it's French.

My face turns red as the substitute tells me to say a little about myself and why I'm taking this class.

What are the vital details that Monsieur LeFleur

needs to know about me? What will impress him? "I'll be a senior at Edison next year, and I'm hoping to graduate early because I want to travel before I start college. And I'm taking this class because I just really enjoy French culture—French history, and French fashion, and French . . . toast." I smile, feeling like an idiot. Then I decide to go on, as if I'm doing an imitation of my mother and need to relate my entire life story. "So for this trip I want to do next spring, before college? I'm hoping maybe France, but definitely Quebec. I actually went to Quebec City and Montreal once, but I was too little to really remember. Except the crepes, I loved the crepes. So then I'm thinking that maybe in college I'll take a semester abroad, so I want to get a lot of practice speaking French before I do that. And then . . ." I notice everyone staring at me. Blankly. "So, I've heard that you're a really great teacher, so get well soon," I conclude. *Just call me Christie Farrell*, I should add.

The substitute turns to Charlotte next. I can't wait to hear her story so I can forget about mine.

"I'm Charlotte," she says. "I mean, *Jeu mappel* Charlotte Duncan. And I'm taking this class because I failed Intermediate Spanish and Intermediate Italian and I've got to pass Intermediate Something. I mean, those are like the rules for graduating at Benjamin Franklin; you can't just take three Beginning classes, even though I personally think it makes a person more well-rounded than two years of only *one* language."

"Ahem." The substitute clears his throat. "Yes, well. Next?"

"I'm here to make up for failing French," the next person says. And the next and the next and the next.

I wonder, is Monsieur LeFleur avoiding our class because all of these people flunked the first time around?

After the introductions are complete, we get ready to watch our video lesson of the day. It's an ongoing story about some students, and we've been watching it the past three classes, but it seems to be a couple of levels above where we are—not to mention a couple of decades old. It involves racing around in small cars and rapid-fire conversations in outdoor cafes. I don't know what's going on until the end of each tape, when they stop to go over the vocabulary words.

"So do you want to do something Saturday before you go to work?" Charlotte leans over to ask me during the video. "Maybe you, me, and Ray could find Steve, and we could all hang out together. Or you, me, and Ray could go to breakfast at IHOP."

"I can't. I'm going to the rink with my dad on Saturday," I say. "Then my parents are going to some lunch thing, so I have to stay home." Finding Steve sounds a lot more interesting.

"Oh. Well, how about Sunday?" she asks.

"I have to help my mom while my dad's at an open house, and then I have to go to the hospital with her for childbirth class," I explain.

"*Ew.* Like, breathing and all that?" she asks.

I nod. "Tell me about it."

"You know what's really gross? Those *movies*—you know, of actual births?"

"What's really gross is that I'm her birth coach," I explain. "I'm going to *be* there when she gives actual birth."

"Triple *ew*," Charlotte says. "Hey, is that French? 'Cause I think that really sounded French."

The substitute walks in just as Charlotte and I are laughing. "Do I need to separate you two?" he comes over and whispers to us.

"No, we'll be quiet," I say.

"Sorry," Charlotte says. "I mean, ex-cue-say *moi*."

As soon as he walks away, Charlotte passes me a note with IHOP = STEVE GROPHER written on it.

As if I could forget that.

Absolute Hams

"**H**e still has it." Dad's coach and choreographer, Ludmila, shakes her head as she watches him out on the ice.

I'm not sure what she's talking about. Does she mean he's had it? Or that he's got it? "Yes," I say, stupidly.

"Your father. It is so amazing. His agility, his strength." Ludmila kisses her fingers. "He might be twenty, not forty."

"He's thirty-nine, actually," I tell her.

She ignores my correction. "He is a young man when he takes the ice," she says.

Dad found Ludmila about six months ago through an ad in a skating magazine. She takes on students from about a two-hundred-mile radius. He only gets to see her once a week, so today is important for him. He ate three energy bars in the car on the drive here just so he would be ready. He has three hours of ice time with her this morning, and then he has to rush back for an open house, while

Mom covers someone's Saturday shift and I once again hang out with Dorothy, Torvill, and Dean until I go to work at three.

"So he's doing that well?" I ask. "I mean, he looks polished to me, but he always did. And he's so critical of himself."

Ludmila shakes her head. "You cannot listen to him. He is crazy. He is insane."

"He is?" I ask. "I mean, I'd sort of suspected." My joke is lost on Ludmila.

"If he makes just one mistake, he does the entire program over," she goes on. "Entire! Entire thing! He is so *demanding*."

And she isn't even in debt to him. "Tell me about it," I say.

I was only being sarcastic, but Ludmila takes me literally and starts to tell me how my father has the strength of a bull and the grace of a large bird. I think she means a swan. "Very unique," she says. "One of a kind."

"So does he have a shot at making the masters tour?" I ask.

"Oh, yes. A shot," she says. "Yes, he does. He has very good shot. Only . . ."

"What?" I ask.

"Don't call us, we'll call you," Ludmila says.

I wait a minute, hoping she will explain this.

"That is how these tours work. They want Olympic

gold, they want world champions. They call on the telephone, please join us. Your father . . ."

"No gold medal, no cereal box," I say.

She nods. "He needs to find a sponsor. To pay his way, to get him more lessons, more ice," she says. "Then it will be a pinch."

"A cinch?" I ask.

But she doesn't hear me. She is calling to my father, something about his takeoff for his combination triple jump.

I can't imagine how my father will find a sponsor in Lindville, but maybe he will. Could he skate with "Gabe's Auto World" stitched onto the back of his shirt?

I watch as he stops his program to work on his triple Axel with Ludmila. He's been doubling it today because he can't quite triple it, which makes sense to me because the Axel is the hardest jump there is. Ludmila shouts instructions to him. I can't understand half of what she says because of her accent.

Dad looks tired, like he'd rather be leafing through an interior design magazine or composing a new house-for-sale listing.

The rink smells like old, wet socks—sort of musty and mothball-like. I don't miss skating at all, I think.

But then I remember skating at the town rink in Lindville one winter, when I was about eight. It was around Christmas, and there were a lot of people skating there, even though it's an outdoor rink and it was freezing cold. Dad and I hadn't skated there very often, because we usually skated here, at the arena.

First we were skating on our own, but then we started skating together. Everyone was watching us and looking sort of amazed. Dad and I did jumps at the same time—totally synchronized—and people started applauding. It wasn't even embarrassing, it was just fun. We improvised this program, on the spot. Dad told me what to do out of the corner of his mouth, and I did it. We totally ate it up. We were absolute hams. We posed for a picture. And after that, we did it occasionally, whenever we wanted to unwind and have fun.

It's something I can't even conceive of doing now. The last time I skated in public was such a disaster. It was like I could hear these imaginary commentators saying, "that'll be another point-four deduction," every time I fell or stepped out of a landing. When I finally finished my program, I skipped the so-called Kiss and Cry area, walked right past my dad, and went straight to "Kiss and Despair."

Come to think of it, I'm not sure if I've ever actually *left*.

Always Tweedledee

"**M**onica?" a woman asks. "Please, can you help me?" She is lying on her back, unable to get up by herself.

"Me, too," another woman pleads. "Uh! I just can't—oof!" She struggles to roll over.

It's like being in a room full of turtles. Not that I've ever been around a turtle—never mind a roomful—but I'm guessing the Lamaze Lounge resembles a tank right about now.

Monica rushes over with a perky smile and gently helps them turn over so that they can climb up on their hands and knees. Childbirth class is so glamorous. We just learned that one of the birth coach's jobs is to remind the mother to pee before she goes into hard labor. "Repeat after me," Monica said. "Don't forget to urinate!"

Childbirth is one of the few adult things that I *can* wait for. Gladly.

"I guess your massage is being cut short today,"

Monica says to the two women. "Unless you want to be each other's partners until your significant others return?"

The women look at each other, consider it for two seconds, and then shake their heads.

"Now, this is why I'm glad you're here with me, Peggy," my mother says as I gently rub her back. I'm tracing little circles, as instructed.

"Why?" I ask.

"Don't you see what's going on? Their husbands went out to get a drink of water and they've been gone for at least fifteen minutes," she says. "And I'll bet you anything they're off in a bar somewhere having a beer." She sounds very bitter, instead of peaceful, the way she's supposed to feel during the massage session.

"Wait a second." My eyes widen. "Is that what Dad did? Is that why you asked me to help you this time?"

"No, of course not," she says.

"Oh." I sigh. That would have been interesting.

"No. But when you were being born in Boston, and I was in labor for sixteen hours, your father went off and had a glass or two of California merlot," Mom continues. "When he came back he had purple wine stains in the corners of his mouth. He tried to tell me it was grape juice from the cafeteria."

"Dad? Really?" I laugh.

"Your father is not like other men," she says with a smile. "However, he is still a man."

I pause for a minute, reflecting on this. "Hey, did you ever scream and yell at him when you were giving birth?" I ask.

"Constantly," she says. "When I had the twins? I told him to go back to the Ice Jubilee and get back into his Tweedledum costume and stay there." She laughs. "Which is so silly, because he was never Tweedledum. He was always Tweedledee."

"He was?" I ask. "I don't remember that."

"You were young. Dorothy's age. It was a traveling show that went bankrupt," Mom says. "Fortunately for us." She takes deep breaths in and out, in and out. "But you know what? Sometimes I wish we were still on the road."

"You do?" I ask.

"Sure. I mean, Lindville's nice and all, but it's not exactly unpredictable. You pretty much know what's going to happen every day."

"True," I agree. How very, very, very true.

"Especially when it comes to the weather," Mom says. "It's sunny, it's hot, it's dry, it's windy. It doesn't rain enough. We don't get good *storms*. You know? I miss predicting storms. That intense, hyped-up feeling at the studio and around-the-clock coverage and telling people stuff that really *matters*." She glances over at the woman who critiqued her errant forecast. "Nothing exciting ever happens, so you stop thinking it's going to. And then something does happen, and you miss it. Completely."

I gaze at my mother with newfound respect. "I know what you mean." I can't believe she has thoughts like this. I thought I was the only one.

"I bet you'll be really glad when you graduate and go off to college," Mom says. "Then I can visit you. It'll be so much fun!"

While she's babbling about all the fun things we can do together, I get this picture of me leaving in a little over a year, standing by the minivan with all my duffel bags and some cardboard boxes with books, and a desk lamp and a clock and my posters. Torvill, Dean, Dorothy, and the new baby are all standing on the doorstep, happily waving good-bye to me as I head off to college. And in the picture, I am completely miserable and everyone else is smiling, and then they realize I'm not smiling and they rush over to hug me.

Maybe I don't want to leave my family and get out of here. But how can I *stay* here? I'm not staying here. I'm *not*.

As I sit there massaging my mother's back, I switch gears and start thinking about my plan to sprint out of Edison High next spring—my pre-college road trip. How am I ever going to pull it off? How am I ever going to get out of my endless list of responsibilities? How will I pay back my parents, get enough credits to graduate, buy a car, and find someone—preferably Steve, but I can't picture him graduating early and I also can't picture my parents allowing me to go on a three-month road trip with a boy—to go with me?

"Peggy?" My mother shifts on her floor mat. "You're rubbing really, really hard."

"Sorry!" I say. "I'll stop." I decide to stop trying to figure out my future, because it's obviously painful for both of us, and start thinking about something a little more amusing. Like Charlotte's idea to streak down the street during the rodeo parade. I picture Steve streaking naked.

Maybe not streaking completely naked, maybe wearing a little something. Like cowboy boots.

With spurs, of course. Definitely spurs.

The Crispest Crisp

At 6:55 A.M. the customers are all complaining to Denny, because gas prices have suddenly spiked fourteen cents. People are talking about politics and getting slightly irate. No one's paying at the pump because they want to come in and personally complain. Denny just keeps repeating, "It's not my fault."

I try to lighten the mood by offering free coffee samples. People glare at me. Then I mention how I fell down that morning trying to get away from the Doberman, and how the dog looked so pleased with himself when I wiped out and landed on my butt.

Denny starts laughing. So does the woman buying cigarettes, a soda, and chocolate cupcakes. I'm glad I can provide some comic relief. It's like some sort of strange cathartic release; gas prices are through the roof, but laugh at the clumsy girl and you'll feel better! We do what we can here at Gas 'n Git.

The truck driver with the minty-fresh breath comes in and is nice to me, and I almost ask him if he'll give me a ride so that I can get out of here. I don't really care where he's going. He could drop me at the next truck stop, and that would be all right.

"You have a nice day now," he says as he stuffs a dollar into the tip tank, and picks up a few wintergreen mints for the road. "Don't let this heat get to you. It'll pass."

I reach up to touch my forehead, which has sweaty bangs sticking to it. I hadn't realized how much the heat was affecting me, or at least my hair. "Thanks," I say, and I smile at him. "You, too."

I'm always saying "You, too" at the wrong moments, when the thing I'm responding to (like "have a nice day now.") is already forgotten. I just told the nicest customer in the world that he would pass, too. But at least I made Denny happy because I said "U2."

After he leaves, I start wondering what's happened to World's Worst Coffee Breath, who is now five minutes past schedule. I can't believe I'm worrying about him.

"Hey, Kristi Yamaguchi. In all seriousness," Denny says when suddenly the store is empty of miffed customers.

"In all seriousness, don't call me Kristi," I say. "That's my mom's name. Spelled differently, but still."

"Okay, then. Miss Farrell. If you want, I can give you

a ride to work some mornings," Denny offers.

"Thanks. I'll keep that in mind," I say. I can just picture my dad's expression as Denny roars into the driveway on his motorcycle at 5 A.M.

Then I notice Mike Kyle, of all people, walking into the store. He's wearing a baseball cap backward and his brown hair is sticking out from underneath. His T-shirt says, **LIVING ON THE EDGE**. He wears cutoff khaki shorts and red flip-flops.

"Hey," he says to me. "I didn't know you worked *this* early." He hands a credit card to Denny. "It's my dad's, he's outside," he explains. "Pump four."

"Okay," Denny says. "You know, we have pay at the pump."

"I know," Mike says.

He looks at me, as if I'm supposed to talk next. So I do.

"So. Did you just finish your paper route?" I ask.

"Nah, I finished it at five-thirty. Now my dad's driving me around to look for a new car."

"Cool. But why this early?" I ask.

"He says we have to scope the lots before the salespeople show up," Mike says. "So we can plan what we're going to offer." He rolls his eyes.

"But you're getting a car," I say, trying not to seethe outright with jealousy. Seething is very unattractive. Why I want to be attractive to Mike, I don't know. Maybe he'll mention to Steve that he saw me, and I wouldn't want to come off as a jealous seether. "Car shopping's a *good* thing," I say. I peer outside at Mike's father. The car at pump four is a teal minivan. Mr. Kyle must not be living on the edge, the way his son is.

"For *him*. He's getting a Corvette. He's trading in the Camaro *and* the van," Mike says as he signs the receipt. "Then he's getting me some cheap old beater."

I shrug. "It's a car. Right?"

"I guess," Mike admits with a shrug. He smiles at me. "Don't look a horse in the mouth when you get a gift and all that, right?"

"I definitely wouldn't look inside any horses' mouths," I say. "Really questionable dental hygiene."

Mike laughs, just as a familiar silver Lexus screeches to a stop in the No Parking zone. Speaking of dental hygiene.

"Now *there's* a nice ride," Mike says. "Well, gotta go, see you!"

After he walks out, Denny turns to me, just as World's Worst Coffee Breath is walking in. "You're not actually . . . friends with that guy. Are you?"

"I don't know," I say. "Why?"

"Let's just say . . . he's not the crispest crisp in the chip bucket." Denny swipes a credit card through the cash register reader.

"What's that supposed to mean? You're mixing your

really bad British metaphors," I tell him.

"Just aspiring to be like your friend Mr. Western Wear," Denny says under his breath.

"Good morning!" World's Worst Coffee Breath greets me as he strides happily up to the counter.

"Hi. The usual?" I smile at him. I quickly pour him a giant Tanker-size cup from the new tank of High Octane Blend. "Did you know we have mint-flavored coffee?" I ask as I ring up his purchase. "Actually, I think it might be mint-chocolate. I'm not totally sure, but I could make some up for you."

"Oh, no, thanks," he says. "I hate flavored coffees. They just get in the way."

"You know, sir," Denny says, coming over to us. "We're having a special today. Buy one coffee, get a pack of spearmint gum for, uh, fifty cents." He holds up a handful of gum.

"That's a special?" Coffee Breath asks.

"Usually gum is sixty-five, so it's a deal," Denny says. "Definitely a deal."

"Hmm. Maybe next time. The special runs for how long?" Coffee Breath asks.

"Indefinitely," Denny says. "*In*definitely a deal is what I should have said, actually."

Coffee Breath laughs, and I turn to Denny and smile before making two lattes for the next customer.

After I finish that, and after Coffee Breath leaves,

Denny and I both rush over to the door, racing each other. We fling it open and stand outside taking huge gulps of fresh air, before we realize this is a big mistake. You don't gulp air here in Lindville. You sip it.

Steve, What's So Funny?

A few days later, I go to meet Charlotte at her Shady Prairies job. She and Ray and I are going to the Lot in search of Steve. Ray doesn't know about the searching-for-Steve part.

I wait in the kitchen while Charlotte goes out to serve her last tray. She walks back into the kitchen with a trayful of untouched dishes of tan goop. "Everyone has to have their butterscotch pudding, except for when they all of a sudden decide they don't like pudding. Then they try to tell you how they've *never* liked butterscotch pudding, which is so ridiculous, because they ate it on Tuesday. But not according to them."

I shrug. "So what do you do?"

"I stand there and tell them they're not allowed to go batty on me, I don't care how old they are."

"How old are they?" I ask.

"Anywhere from sixty-five to a hundred," Charlotte

says. "I have this one table, my favorite table, of old ladies who are ninety plus. They still dress up for dinner and they have like, drinks first, and then after dessert they go outside and smoke, even though this entire area is supposed to be a No Smoking zone. I love them."

"They sound fun. But you know what's weird?" I say. "Why don't they move to Phoenix or Miami, or somewhere else where everyone retires, somewhere that's a little more glamorous? You know what I mean?"

"They must like it here," Charlotte says as she scrapes uneaten butterscotch pudding into the garbage can. Clumps of it cling to the side of the trash bag.

"So is that how long it takes to like Lindville? Sixty-five *years*?" I joke.

Charlotte and I look at each other and start laughing.

"I don't think I can wait that long. I mean, I really don't," I say.

After Charlotte finishes serving all her tables, we go to find Ray, who's a dishwasher. He goes to Edison, like me, and is usually hanging out with Steve's crowd, so Charlotte and I decided the four of us are meant to hang out this summer.

"This is Fleming," Charlotte introduces me.

"Yeah, I know," Ray says. "Hey." He runs a hand through his short black hair, and I check out his arms. They are definitely nice—why hadn't I ever noticed before? Ray takes off his dirty apron and tosses it into a plastic hamper. "So, we going to the Lot?" Ray puts his arms around Charlotte.

"Where else?" Charlotte says, snuggling up to him.

"I don't know. I was thinking maybe L.A. New York. Omaha," I say.

Charlotte laughs. "Yeah, okay, Fleming. Whatever you say."

An hour later, I'm at the Lot sitting on the tailgate of Ray's pickup with Charlotte, Ray, and Mike. Steve and Jacqui are a few cars away, leaning against someone's old convertible, inseparable once again.

This is so not how it was supposed to be.

There are clouds covering the sky, and whenever there are clouds at night, they trap the air here. It might be gorgeous and sunny and breezy all day, and you'd forget you were in the Penned Cattle Capital of the World. Then it gets cloudy, a few drops of rain spit from the sky, and suddenly the air sinks down over the town like a collapsing hot-air balloon.

But the smelly night is the least of my problems.

Mike has been telling Ray about his new car for about ten minutes. I haven't really been listening, though I did hear it was a yellow Geo Metro with 180,000 miles on it and a purple Princess sticker that he hasn't been able to pry off the bumper.

Charlotte and I were doing our French homework

until we lost daylight. We tried to tell Mike and Ray that we were conjugating verbs and they started making jokes about conjugal visits and we haven't really wanted to talk to them since.

But now Mike gives up talking to Ray and turns to me. "So what kind of air freshener do you think I should get?" he asks.

"Air freshener?" I ask.

"For the car. The person who had it before was like a serious smoker," Mike says. "I've got to kill that smell."

I start to smile, glad that Mike and I at least have something in common. We both hate stink. But then, who doesn't? "Well, what are your options?"

"I'm trying to decide between new car and strawberry," Mike says.

"Hmm." I was thinking more along the lines of tropical breeze. "I'd go for new car," I say. "For the irony factor."

Mike looks a little confused. "But I really like strawberry," he says.

"Well." I shrug. Strawberry seems kind of feminine, but whatever—I really don't care. "You could always get both," I tell him. "But then your car might *really* stink."

"Yeah," he says with a laugh. "Maybe I'll just leave the windows down for a while. It'll be easy with my new job, because it's going to be hot and I don't have A/C."

"What's your new job? Delivering pizza or something?" I ask. I've been down that road before—and crashed.

Mike's face falls. "Yeah. How did you guess?"

"Sorry. It was just the one job I really associate with driving. Which place are you working for?"

"Smiley's," he says.

I nod. "I worked for Bob's—last spring," I say.

"Really? Cool."

"Yeah. But I didn't last very long," I say.

"You hated it?" Mike says.

"Something like that." I smile, deciding not to tell him about the unglamorous crash I had. I might want to borrow his car someday or something.

What am I saying? The lack of pure oxygen must be affecting my brain. Like I'd ever borrow Mike's car. Then again, I never thought I'd be sitting on a tailgate next to him, either.

I glance over at Steve. He's the one I'm supposed to be sitting next to. This is all wrong.

"So, uh, when do you start?" I ask Mike.

"Tomorrow," Mike says, sounding a little more proud now.

"So I won't see you on the bus anymore? You're leaving me to perish with Kamikaze Driver at the wheel?" I put my hand to my throat. "How could you?"

Mike laughs. "Sorry. Is that what you call him?"

"Among other things." I take a sip of my root beer. I glance over at Charlotte, who now has one leg thrown over Ray's. I check to see whether Steve and Jacqui have moved an inch away from each other yet. Nope.

I hate being in this type of situation. Where there are couples all around you hooking up, and you're so obviously not. When you don't know someone very well, and you're trying to make conversation and it's impossible. When you have to be home by 10:00.

As I'm staring at Steve, I notice Mike is kind of looking at me, observing my obsession. I don't want him telling Steve that I was staring, so I turn to him and blurt out, "You should have seen him today. Kamikaze. He was so obsessed with making every light. I swear he was counting them down out loud, as he went through each green or yellow light. There might have been some red ones in there—after a while I stopped looking because I didn't want to know."

"He's the kind of person who's going to be arrested, and then everyone will say, yeah, he seemed really weird," Mike says. "You know what I mean?"

"Yeah." I stare at Steve and Jacqui. They're entwined, like an exotic plant.

Why did she have to show up here this summer? Why did she have to ruin my plan? It wasn't much of a plan, but it was in development. Now it's dead.

"Hey, um, Peg?" Mike gently pushes his fingers

120

against my thigh. I feel these strange shivers travel up my spine when he touches me. "Whoa. You've got really strong muscles," he says.

"It's, um, from skating," I say as goose bumps break out on my arms. "In-line."

"Fleming skates everywhere," Charlotte says.

Except on the ice, I think.

"She's amazingly good. Me, I can hardly make it around the block," Charlotte goes on, but I can't talk to her right now for some reason. I can't stop looking at Mike's hand, which looks strange just perched there on my thigh. What is he doing?

"You know what?" Mike says to me, giving my leg a little squeeze.

"What?" I say, sort of softly, because I feel really close to him all of a sudden.

"I'm *starving*," Mike says. "Let's grab Gropher and hit the Hamburger, okay?" He slides off the truck tailgate.

That wasn't exactly what I was expecting him to say.

Five minutes later, the four of us are sitting in the Happy Hamburger drive-thru—me and Mike in the front seats, Jacqui and Steve wedged into the backseat of the Geo, on top of each other. This is not the double date I had in mind. In fact, this is worse than the one I was on five minutes ago.

I order small fries and a lemonade. Jacqui and Steve

split a concrete shake and a double hamburger and large fries, like they're incapable of ordering on their own. They have to share the ketchup and the mustard and the bun or they might self-destruct. I am probably jealous only because Steve and I never actually managed to have a meal together—our relationship wasn't deep enough for that. But we did share spilled ketchup, which is a lot more intense than people might realize.

Mike parks in the Happy Hamburger parking lot, which seems kind of stupid when we could drive anywhere. Steve and Jacqui are eating and slurping their shake. It's a little more than I can take. I always thought the reason Steve and I didn't really go out was because he didn't want to go out with anyone long-term. But he seems okay with seeing Jacqui night after night, so why not me?

I glance over at Mike, who's staring at me for no reason. "So. Um. I think I need a refill," I say, shaking the ice in the bottom of my lemonade cup. This is my lame attempt to prolong the night. Why do I want to prolong agony, I wonder?

"No problem," he says with a nice smile. He reaches over and squeezes my leg again. Then he peels around the parking lot and we approach the speaker with a loud screech.

"I'll order," Steve says. "Pull up, Kyle, pull up!"

The car lurches forward as Mike holds on to the

clutch a little too long, because he just got the car and isn't used to it yet. Then he starts doing it on purpose, inching forward, jerking and bucking the car.

"May I take your order?" a voice asks from the black speaker box.

"Can we get . . . can we get . . ." Steve stammers. He and Mike both start laughing so hard that neither of them can order.

"Hello?" the voice says.

"How about a new clutch?" Steve finally asks. "With fries?"

Mike peels away from the speaker and we fly past the drive-thru window, all of us laughing hysterically—except Jacqui.

"What's so funny?" Jacqui asks. "Steve, what's so funny?"

She's the kind of person who's never cracked up for no reason at a drive-thru before. I don't know what Steve sees in her.

I glance in the rearview mirror at Steve as I laugh and he suddenly leans forward and says, "I can't believe I did that, I can't believe I just did that, why did I just do that?" He smiles at me and for a second I feel like there's no one else in the car.

I smile back at him. At first I'm really flattered because he remembers, and because I think about him whispering it in my ear as he kissed me.

Then I'm mad because it was something he used to say to me in private, because it was our thing, and now he's saying it in front of his new girlfriend. I'm thinking, *I can't believe* he *just did that*.

Call Me Cinder-Peggy

"P. F., you are an hour late," my father says sternly when I get home. He looks at his watch. "Correction. An hour and twenty-five minutes late."

"Oh," I say. "Am I? I'm sorry—I didn't realize." However, I did realize that when we left the Lot, it was almost 11:00—making me an hour late. But I was just having such a good time, watching Steve and Jacqui split that last French fry.

"I worry about you!" my father says. "Do you know how many terrible things could happen to you on your way home at eleven-thirty at night on Rollerblades?"

I raise my eyebrows. If he feels that way, then why won't he let me drive? "I was perfectly safe. I was with friends." Of course, neither one of these statements is totally true. But "I was with some boys who drive crazy and drive *me* crazy" wouldn't be the answer to give him right now.

"You were hanging out at that . . . *lot*, weren't you?" he says in a disapproving tone.

"Yes," I say. "Dad, it's where everyone hangs out."

"Yeah, well," he says. "That doesn't make it okay."

"You should be glad I don't hang out with the cemetery crowd," I tell him.

"There's a cemetery crowd? Which cemetery?" Dad asks.

"Eastman. There's the Lot crowd, and then there's the Plot crowd," I tell him.

"You live to worry me, don't you?" He closes the door behind me. "I really wish you hadn't told me that."

"Sorry," I say. "Just trying to keep you informed." I open the fridge and get out a carton of orange juice.

"You've got the early shift tomorrow," he says, eyeing the juice as if it's a dangerous stimulant. "Are you going to be up in time?"

"Dad, I'll be fine." I pour juice into a giant plastic cup with LINDVILLE SAVINGS & LOAN on the side—another of Mom's freebies, as she calls them. I hate the word *freebies*.

"Look, P. F., I'm begging you. Please don't be so late next time, okay?"

What about the fact that he and Mom are late every single time they're supposed to come home and take over watching the kids? "Dad, it's summer, and I'm only taking one class, and nobody else has to be home by ten. I don't even get out of work until eleven on Saturday nights."

"Be home by eleven then," Dad says. "Fine. Eleven. But I need your help with something."

He needs my help? What could I do that I'm not already doing? "What." I don't say it as a question because I don't want to know the answer. I imagine more watching the kids, or maybe something new, like all the laundry instead of just some, or some new housecleaning or cooking assignments. Call me Cinder-Peggy. "Dad, I'm pretty much extended already."

"But this is something different—and fun. It's a skating thing."

I raise my eyebrows. Skating . . . different and fun? Since when?

He looks at the calendar on the refrigerator, nearly buried under Dean's drawings and Torvill's latest sticker attack. "I don't have much time to pull this together. It's coming up in about three weeks. So let me ask you something, and don't say no right away—just hear me out."

"It's about skating? Then no—right away," I say.

"P. F., come on." Dad laughs. "Cut me some slack here. Is there any way at all you'd consider getting back into skating? Just for a onetime thing? Just to help me out?"

"Why, is it Take Your Daughter to Skate Day at the rink or something?" I ask.

Dad laughs. "Very funny. No. It would be you and me

and . . . well, I don't know all the details yet. This is new to me, but someone wants me to perform and I just thought . . . P. F. and I could do this together."

Why on earth would he think that? I've told him so many times that I'm not interested in figure skating anymore.

"See, you and Mom have your childbirth class together and that's great, but I miss hanging out with you, too," he says. "And when the new baby comes, we're going to be even busier, so—I just wanted for us to do something together."

I really appreciate the sentiment, but there's no way I'm doing this, whatever it is. "Dad, there are a hundred reasons I can't help you with some skating thing," I say. "I don't have time to practice, for one. I'm working, remember? And watching the kids, and—"

"Okay, okay. So maybe you'd have to cut your Gas 'n Git hours a little to fit in some rehearsal time. And because you'd be doing that to help me, I'd forgive some of your debt because your paychecks wouldn't be as high. Whatever. We'd work it out."

I don't like the sound of this. He seems a little desperate. "Dad, come on. I told you. I don't want to skate in public, ever again—are you crazy?" Anyway, don't I do enough around here, without helping Dad's skating career, too?

"But you've *been* skating. Every day."

"That's completely different, Dad. And anyway, what is this *for*?"

He isn't giving out any specifics. "It's not for competition; it's strictly for entertainment. You and I would make up the program. You wouldn't have to do anything complicated—I just want it to be fun."

"Fun," I repeat.

"Yes, fun," he says.

We reach a stalemate where neither of us budges or says anything for a minute. I can't believe he's even asking me this. He knows I'm no good anymore.

Then he says, "Your spins were so nice," still pushing the idea. This is how he sells so many houses. He wears people down.

"You can have another protégé or whatever when Dorothy gets older," I tell him. Torvill and Dean have already tried skating and shown exactly zero interest in pursuing it. "Heck, don't even wait. Put her on skates now. Put *her* in your program."

Dad stares out the kitchen window at the street, as if he's considering it. He's juggling a silver Monopoly-size house in his hand, his reward for being a top agent one year. "I don't want Dorothy to skate with me. I want you to, P. F."

"Sorry," I say, "but no. And please don't ask me

again. I mean it, Dad."

"Okay, but I think you'll be sorry," he says as he drops the little house onto the floor and it skids under the fridge.

Somehow I know that I won't be.

So Sorry, Fleming

"**M**onsieur LeFleur is feeling much better," the fifth substitute teacher of the summer tells us at our next class.

"So is he coming?" Charlotte asks.

"*Mais non,*" the substitute says. "He was ready to return today, but there has been a death in the family."

There's a giant, collective sigh. It's like waiting for a rock concert to start, and then being told that the headliner's bus broke down on the highway. Monsieur LeFleur is kind of like that to us, at least by reputation. A rock star. Letting his fans down.

We had been making Monsieur LeFleur a giant, poster-size get-well card covered with French phrases. We now set that aside and begin our sympathy card. Nobody can agree on what to draw or say first.

Charlotte picks up a black marker and draws a smiley face with the smile upside down and a bunch of notches in the frown. It looks like a warning for poison.

We can't stop laughing. I know it's wrong and disrespectful, but I can't.

"You know what? We need more info if we're going to do this right. So who died?" Rafael, one of my classmates, asks.

"*Pardonnez moi?*" the substitute asks. "*Répétez en français.*" Only a few of our substitutes know French, and so far they've all been posers. Their knowledge expires after about five minutes—or five sentences, whichever comes first.

"Uh . . ." Rafael pauses. "*Mourir?*" he says. "*Famille?*"

"I still don't understand," the sub says. "*Je ne comprends pas.*"

"In his family. Who *died?*" Rafael demands, sounding angry now. "I mean, what are we supposed to write?"

"*Je ne sais pas.*" The sub shrugs. "Use your imagination. Be creative."

"What does that phrase mean again?" Charlotte asks me. "*Ne sais . . . ?*" She really should not be in Intermediate French, because this is one of the first things we learned in Beginning French, but somehow I sense it won't matter in this class.

"It means 'I don't know,'" I tell her. I write it down for her.

Charlotte starts writing. "On the loss of your *je ne sais pas.*" She turns to me as she pushes the card across the table.

"That has some French in it, so it counts," she tells me.

As the card gets passed around class, I open up my book and my dictionary and try to compose the perfect sympathy message. Monsieur LeFleur has been going through a terrible time lately. I want to tell him how bad I feel about all this.

The card is handed back to me last and there isn't any room left for me to write anything except, "So sorry, Fleming." In English.

When I walk out of the school, Mom is waiting in the minivan for me. Charlotte and I had planned to hit IHOP, but Mom insists I go bed shopping with her, Dean, Torvill, and Dorothy. This is because she knows she can't keep track of them *and* buy a bed at the same time.

"I had plans, Mom," I tell her as Charlotte and I stand beside the minivan.

"Sorry, Peggy." This seems to be the theme of the afternoon. "This is the only afternoon we can do this."

"There must be other afternoons," I say. "What about Dad? Why doesn't Dad go bed shopping?"

"Peggy, please. I'm really not in the mood."

Like I am? I look at Charlotte. "Sorry."

"Call me later," she says. "And don't worry, Steve isn't doing anything except spilling eggs on other people."

I laugh. "Yeah, you're right."

"Who's Steve?" my mother asks as I get into the minivan and pull on my seat belt.

"Just this guy from school we know," I tell her.

"Steve, Steve, Steve!" Torvill chants from the backseat.

"*Shh!*" I tell her. I don't know who would overhear us, seeing as how the windows are closed and the A/C is on, but it's a conditioned response.

"Do they make lambs there?" Dean asks from the backseat as we drive past a large sign for Majestic Lamb Company. On it, there's a picture of a small, very cute white lamb.

"No. They actually make lambs into lamb *chops* there," I say.

"Cool!" Dean says, kicking the back of my seat for emphasis.

"Peggy." Mom scolds me instead of him.

"Well, it's true," I say. "They process lambs."

"They're too young to hear about that now," Mom whispers as she makes a left. "What were you thinking? Come on, Peggy, *try* to think of someone besides yourself."

This has to be an ironic comment. Doesn't it?

Ten minutes later, we are standing in Sleep City, in front of a maze of cribs and bunk beds. Mom is considering purchasing something called a Funky Bunk, which has a metal frame and ladder with bright orange and purple tiger-stripe patterns on it. Dorothy, Dean, and Torvill are playing with blocks over in the kids' play area. The strip mall we're in is known for its sub sandwich shop, and it's weird to look at beds and smell baking bread and melting cheese.

The salesman, who looks about two years older than me, has decided to give us "some moments to decide," because Mom wouldn't stop telling him what a hard time she's having sleeping through the night with her big belly and how she can't get comfortable and asking him for mattress recommendations.

I see him over at his desk, eating a sub from next door for lunch and eyeing us carefully, as if we're going to walk out with a crib while he's chewing his cold-cut special. Or maybe he's just worried that Mom's going to go over and start discussing water retention again.

Mom keeps wandering around, rubbing her giant pregnant belly, describing things like a math logic problem with no solution. "Let's see. Dorothy could move in with Torvill, so then the baby could move into Dorothy's nursery. . . . Then Dean can move into that small room at the end of the hall—"

"Mom, that's a closet," I say.

"No, it isn't. We just use it as a closet. It's actually quite large," Mom says, sounding a little defensive.

"No, it isn't. It's not big enough for Dean. But look—he can have my room," I say. "I'll move up to the attic."

"What? No! Peggy, no." Mom shakes her head. "I will not have you living in the attic."

"The basement then," I say, though the second I suggest this I regret it, because the basement has a damp, forgotten-laundry smell that will seep into my clothes, my skin, my life. "No, the attic. And Mom, it won't be for long—I'll be leaving next year, anyway," I remind her.

Suddenly she starts bawling, right in the middle of Sleep City. Her face is pink and puffy and she sinks onto a rollaway bed with her head in her hands, and the bed screeches as it rolls under her weight.

I glance over at the salesman, who's staring at us, an onion slice hanging from his lip. He immediately looks away, embarrassed.

What's the matter? I want to say. *Haven't you ever seen a woman who's nine months pregnant break down before?*

"Mom, it'll be okay," I say, my throat tickling with emotion. I put my hand on her shoulder and she grips it tightly, making me worry about how hard she's going to squeeze me during her labor.

"I don't want you to leave," she manages to get out between crying gulps.

I feel like I'm about to start crying, too. This is bizarre because I don't cry in public, and I don't want to start now.

136

"I . . . what am I going to do without you?" my mother wonders out loud.

The way she says it, I can't tell if she's talking about missing me . . . or missing all my help.

I open her purse and hand her a tissue. Then I go and tell the salesman we'll take the Funky Bunk.

It's Only Lindville

It's Friday night, I've just finished making dinner for Dorothy, Torvill, and Dean, and am rushing to get ready to go out when my parents finally come home from the mall. Mom had a fit this morning and decided she finally needed actual and brand-new maternity clothes for her ninth month. Now I won't even have time to take a shower before Mike picks me up. I hate that.

I brush my hair, replace my spaghetti-sauce-stained white T-shirt with a black tank, pull on clean shorts, and quickly put on some mascara and lip gloss. I brush on some blush, too. Working at Gas 'n Git is not exactly helping to create a sun-drenched summer look.

I run downstairs and almost lose one of my black slides and wipe out on the way. When I regain my balance at the bottom of the stairs, I see my father sitting in the living room, taking Western clothing out of familiar-looking red plastic bags and laying them on the sofa.

There is country music on the stereo.

This isn't exactly a typical evening for Phil Farrell. What's going on? I wonder as I look at the gingham shirts, bandanas, jeans with a rope belt, and brown suede pants with fringe.

"Is that stuff from Western Wear Bonanza?" I ask, incredulous.

"Yes," Dad says. "Mr. Stinson wants me to evaluate them."

"Evaluate?" I ask. "Why would you want to?" My father's style is definitely not Western.

"I need a costume. They've asked me to put something together for the Rodeo Roundup Days. Mr. Stinson's on the board of directors, so he's outfitting me." Dad picks up a red gingham shirt and holds it against himself. "I know you won't skate with me, but could you help me figure something out? Am I a red gingham or a blue gingham kind of guy?"

"Um . . . *neither*? Dad, I don't understand." Or maybe I just don't *want* to understand. I'm getting this horrible sinking feeling. "You don't mean . . . skating at the rodeo. Do you?"

He nods.

I can't believe this. *"That's* where you wanted me to skate with you?" My father must not be getting enough sleep. He's going insane or something. Like I'd ever skate with him at a rodeo? In what universe?

He nods and then he loops a bolo tie around his neck and tries to shorten it. "They're trying to bring in different types of events this year, to attract a wider audience," Dad explains. "And if this goes well, there's a chance that Mr. Stinson and some others will sponsor me for my comeback. They very strongly hinted that they'd support me, if I helped them out with this."

I can't believe what I'm hearing. The plan is insane. "Excuse me. Dad? Ice skating? Where are they going to *do* this? It'll be ninety degrees—in the shade. We can barely keep ice frozen in the freezer in July."

"Listen, I'm with you, P. F. I told them it's not going to work, especially when we only have three weeks to prepare, but they begged me. They're converting the town rink—you know it's right next to the fairgrounds. They're closing it off and air-conditioning it. And they're bringing in a walk-in meat freezer expert from Majestic—they say he knows how to keep the surface frozen. If it's good enough for steak, it's good enough for me. *I* don't know."

"*Dad*. If it doesn't work . . . your reputation . . ."

"It's only Lindville," he says as he sets a black ten-gallon hat on his head. "And they're going to pay me. Quite a bit of money, actually."

"But Dad, you don't have to do this," I say. "You're *good*. You're an *artist*."

"P. F., I've worn smelly fur costumes and dressed as cartoon characters. I've played Tweedledee. Being in the

Rodeo Roundup Days isn't *that* much of a stretch." He takes off the black hat and throws it onto the sofa with a flourish. "P. F., there comes a time when everyone has to—"

"Make sacrifices," I finish the sentence for him, then sigh. "Okay, but *this* one?" It's going to be so embarrassing. My father is talking about skating at the rodeo. And he's actually going to do it.

"Peggy, you know what they say. Every cloud has a silver lining." Dad yanks off the bolo tie and throws it on the coffee table, then walks out of the living room.

Even Lindville clouds? I wonder.

I pick up a suede vest and hold it up against me, inhaling its leather smell. I try to picture my father skating with Justin boots fashioned into skates. I try to picture the two of us out there, together. My mind goes blank.

A car honks outside, and I drop the vest as if it's radioactive.

"Be home by ten!" my father calls from the kitchen as I hurry out the door.

"Eleven!" I yell over my shoulder as the door closes.

"What's *your* favorite thing about the rodeo?" Mike asks me as he parks the Geo under a sign in front of the stadium that says RODEO FANS ONLY.

We're in the middle of what will soon be rodeo bedlam. Right now it's empty booths, banners announcing different events, and chained-off areas ready for petting zoos and carnival rides.

"The day it's over," I say as Steve, Jacqui, and I climb out of the car. *Especially this year*, I think as I notice the skating rink on the other end of the stadium, which looks like a construction zone with tarps and scaffolding. Ray and Charlotte are parking right beside us, in Ray's pickup—we all met up at the Lot about five minutes ago.

"What are they doing to the rink?" Steve asks, apparently following my gaze.

"Closing it off, because—" I start to explain, then stop. I don't want to tell everyone about this—I don't want anyone except Charlotte to know. "Actually I'm not really sure what they're doing," I say.

We head for the picnic tables already set up for the food concessions, with two pizzas that Mike brought from work. There must be about a hundred tables.

I don't know how I feel about this. I get to hang out with Steve, but only if I do it when Jacqui and Mike are there. It's like a very sorry logic equation on the SAT. The answer to "What do I like about this?" is "None of the above."

I wonder if Steve gets jealous seeing me with Mike. I hope he does. Not that there's anything between me and Mike, but if I can make Steve think there is . . . maybe he'll feel as terrible seeing us together as I do when I see Steve and Jacqui. Maybe he'll come to my rescue the way he did at that St. Patrick's Day party.

Somehow I doubt it, but isn't it worth a shot, at this point? Nothing else seems to be working, and we are constantly being thrown together on this awkward pseudo—double date.

"You know what I like?" Steve says. "I like seeing all the RVs and horse trailers and amusement rides pulling out of town. Because then we get the town back."

"Hmm. Do we *want* the town back?" I joke.

Steve starts to laugh, and I look at him and think, *You know, we could be having this much fun, like, all the time. If only you'd get rid of the girl with the plastic facial features and no brain.*

"Wouldn't we rather be *in* the trailers, leaving?" I ask Steve.

"Definitely. Stowaways." Steve grins at me. "But I don't know if we want to go cross-country with horses."

So he does remember what we talked about, our vague plan to pull a Jack Kerouac.

"You're riding across the country on horseback?" Jacqui asks, coming up beside Steve and taking his hand.

"No," Steve says, shaking his head.

"Then what?" she asks.

"Never mind," Steve says. "It's not important."

Yes, it is! I want to scream. *It's incredibly, vitally, excruciatingly important. And you are letting Jacqui get in the way of all of it.*

I walk over toward Charlotte.

"Does the parade wind up here, at the end?" she asks me. "And then everyone parades around the stadium over there?"

"Usually," I say. "It goes down Main Street and then—wait a second. You're not still planning to be in the parade, are you?"

"Of course I am," she says. "You're still thinking about it, too, aren't you?"

"No!" I glance ahead at Steve, remembering the streaking conversation at IHOP, and how embarrassed he got. "I mean, sure, I'm *thinking* about it," I lie loudly, hoping he'll hear me and be impressed. "But I'm not sure I'm going to do it," I tell Charlotte. One major humiliation in the family during Rodeo Roundup Days is enough.

"You're not?" Charlotte asks. "Not even if I can find a way for us to escape afterward?"

"We'd have to escape really, really far away," I say.

"What are you guys getting away from?" Mike asks, tuning into our conversation as he opens the top pizza box and tears off a slice. Suddenly everyone is looking at us; everyone is tuned in.

"We need to get away from a situation," Charlotte says. "Well, not now, but a few weeks from now. We'll need to be picked up and whisked away."

"Don't keep saying *we*. I'm not doing it," I tell Charlotte. I glance over at Steve. I'm not sure if he remembers Charlotte talking about streaking, that day at IHOP.

He may have blocked it out.

"You're doing it, Fleming," Charlotte insists. "It's going to be the highlight of the rodeo."

"*What* is?" Mike asks. "What are you guys doing? Barrel racing or something?"

"Or something," I say.

"Whatever. You guys are weird," Ray says.

"Thank you," Charlotte says.

We all wander around, waiting for someone to pick a table for us to sit down at.

"My favorite part of the rodeo is the games," Steve says. "I could play those all day. I will, actually."

"I thought you quit gambling," Jacqui says.

"Hey, shooting at a metal duck is not gambling. Throwing a dart at a balloon is not gambling," Steve says.

"Yeah, they don't give you any money," Mike points out. "Just stuffed animals, and how many of those can you use?"

"You'd be surprised. Last year I donated about twenty to the hospital for kids," Steve says.

I am about to tell him how cool that is when Jacqui grabs Steve's arm with both her hands. "That's so incredible," she says. "Wow."

"Not really. They were pink and blue and they smelled funny," Steve says.

"Still," Jacqui insists, tugging at Steve the way Dorothy tugs at me when I'm on the phone and she wants attention.

Steve suddenly decides we should sit at the table that's right in the middle of all of them. He and Jacqui sit on one side, while Mike perches across from them. I sit down next to Mike, scooting a little closer to him than may be necessary. When Steve sees me getting close to Mike, his jealousy will have to kick in, the way mine kicked in weeks ago when I saw him kissing Jacqui. Not that I'm going to kiss Mike. But we are spending time together—and that has to get to Steve eventually. Doesn't it? *Kick in, kick in, kick in*, I think, as if I'm Torvill. *Please*.

But nothing seems to get to Steve, because when he and Jacqui are together they create this disgusting force field of happiness that rebuffs any approaches. Especially mine.

I gaze across the table at Steve as I eat a slice of pizza and try to ignore the fact that Mike has slipped off his flip-flops and is trying to play footsie with me. Not that there's anything wrong with that. He's good-looking and he has nice feet. But still, this has to go down as one of the worst Friday nights in history.

I found out my father's going to embarrass me in public, and that Steve still wants to be with Jacqui and not me.

They've both got to be considered insane.

Protection

Denny taps a book of matches against the glass-top sales counter. It's been a slow Saturday night, so slow that we've run out of things to talk about and for some reason I feel compelled to confide in him about my dad's rodeo plan. After we have a good laugh about that, we start discussing our work history, the jobs we've loved, the jobs we've hated, the jobs we've lost.

"So, okay, can I ask you something?" I say. "Why aren't you working at a music store? Or a CD store? I mean, that seems more like where you'd want to work."

"You're a genius. You know that, right?" Denny snaps.

"Hey, forget I asked." I start to walk away.

Denny doesn't say anything for a few minutes, and I'm kind of glad. Talk about a short fuse.

Then he walks over to me. "Remember how I said people end up here? Because of something that happened, because they have a story?"

I nod. "Sure."

"Okay. So, of course I used to work at a music store," Denny says. "I mean, come on. I worked at the stupid Disc Barn for like a year."

"In the mall?" I ask. I can't picture it. "You?"

"Yes, me," Denny says. "But I was too opinionated. I kept telling people they shouldn't buy stuff," Denny says, "and I couldn't stop, not even after the manager told me to. Like if someone was buying a really awful CD by a good band, or anything by a horrible band, or anything I didn't like. Which is a lot of things. Anyway, so about a year ago I got into this confrontation with this guy about which band was going to be considered more influential in like a hundred years."

"Let me guess. You said U2. And he said . . . ?"

"Velvet Underground. I was shelving discs in the U-V-W section. And I told him, I know Velvet Underground is really, really important—they're crucial—and I could see his point, but I said U2 is just as crucial, and then he said *Zooropa* was crap and called Bono a bleeding heart, just because he happens to be involved in the most important humanitarian causes on the planet—" Denny's voice gets strained so he stops himself, shaking his head. "Anyway, it turned into a huge fistfight. And he won, and I got fired." Denny points to his nose. "This used to be straight, okay?"

I start laughing. "Okay. Wow."

"But working here? How can I have an opinion on what kind of potato chips people want, or whether they should get Regular or Premium gas, or the Silver carwash or the Gold? I mean, I *really* don't care."

"Good point," I say.

"So then I can save my brain for my time off. And my writing." Denny opens his leather bag and starts to show me a notebook filled with lyrics and poetry. Of course, for all I know it could be copied U2 lyrics, or lists of Bono's favorite colors and foods and some of his best quotes, but I'm thinking it's original material and I'm about to tell Denny that I'm impressed, when we both hear tires squealing outside. We look up and see a car screeching out onto the highway.

Denny swears and takes off from behind the counter, and sprints out the door. He comes back a minute later, panting. "Another drive-off," he says, as if he has to explain. He picks up the phone and calls Jamie and then the police to report the theft. While he talks on the phone, I make a fresh tank of decaf for a couple on a date, who ordered and then went over to the circular beef jerky display to make out.

Denny slams down the telephone. "I *hate* drive-offs." He stares out the window for a few minutes. "And I hate Saturday nights," he says. "They're never what you think they're going to be."

"Really," I say in agreement as I deliver the decafs to the happy couple while Denny turns up the radio really loud and sits down behind the register, munching on a bag of fried pork rinds.

My father comes to pick me up from work at 11:15. He knocks on the locked door, and when I look out, I see he's wearing skin-tight workout pants and a sleeveless muscle T-shirt. He waves at me and smiles and then gulps from his sports drink. He looks like a runner who's just finished a marathon—especially with the giant brace over one knee.

"So there's my dad—I guess I won't need a ride after all," I tell Denny, grabbing my courier bag from under the counter. "But thanks."

"That's your dad?" Denny asks. "The guy who's going to skate at the rodeo?" He peers outside as he shuts down the last lights. "Interesting. He reminds me of a young Robin Cousins. No, wait. Toller Cranston maybe."

I stop with my hand on the door. "How do you know all these skating names?" He's kind of freaking me out.

"My mom's obsessed. She keeps saying there ought to be a skating *channel*, okay?"

I laugh, say good night to Denny, and head outside.

"Sorry, P. F.," my father says. "I was down at the arena working on some choreography for my new long program and I lost track of time."

"That's okay," I say.

Dad pops open the car doors and we climb in. "I'm really glad that robber started hitting other towns," he says as he peers out the tinted window. "I'm also glad you don't have the graveyard shift."

"Dad, this place closes at eleven. There is no graveyard shift," I say.

"Still." He looks nervously around the station and at the dark shadows by the Dumpster. He nearly jumps as Denny roars out from beside the darkened store on his motorcycle. Denny pauses to nod to me, then peels out like someone in a fifties movie—Marlon Brando maybe, but with a crooked nose.

Dad locks all the doors. "I don't like the looks of this place at night."

"Dad, that was my coworker," I say. "Denny."

My father clears his throat. "Are you sure you don't want to be our full-time baby-sitter for the summer instead?"

Like I'm not now? I think. "Yes, I'm sure," I say.

"Well. If anything . . . *untoward* ever happened at this place . . . you'd tell me, wouldn't you?" Dad asks as we pull out of the station.

"Of course," I say. "But don't worry, it's pretty tame."

"What about that thief? The criminal holding up gas stations. You have protection, right?"

The last time my father mentioned protection, he and

Mom were giving me a sex talk. "You mean . . . a gun?"

"No! I mean security. They've told you, right—just give a thief all the money. Save yourself."

"Sure thing, Dad. We went over it in training," I tell him. Anyway, if anything happens, Denny's going to spring into action—he's promised me. "You know what? The biggest problem is this mean dog that runs after me every morning on my way to work."

"What? You're kidding. That's horrible," Dad says.

"You know what? If you'd let me drive again, we could buy a really cheap car, and I could use it just to get to work. I have this friend who got an old Geo Metro for practically nothing. Then you wouldn't have to pick me up, and I wouldn't have to skate past scary dogs."

"P. F., you haven't exactly proved you're responsible yet. You still have some work to do on that front." Dad looks both ways and then peels out onto County Highway 87, barely missing a car coming toward us.

This is the man who's telling me about being responsible? "What are you talking about? That's all I'm doing—being responsible," I say.

"I wouldn't say that. I mean, you come home late at night, you won't skate with me, you don't offer to help your mother—"

"Offer? Dad, I get *asked* to help so much that I never get the *chance* to offer. And you're constantly late yourself—like tonight!" I point out.

"P. F., that's not the same thing, and you know it," he says.

I stare out the window. I really do not want to have this argument, not now. I want to pretend this is not happening. I'm not getting picked up from my gas-station coffee-shop job by my father, who's skating in a rodeo. This isn't my life. It can't be.

Free Ride

When I get on the Lindvillager after work four days later, it seems like a normal day, except that Denny was out sick and I had to work with Jamie instead, which was a little nerve-wracking. She kept insisting that I clean out all the machines and tubes so that the coffee would flow better and the "turbo dispense" function would work. And she kept insisting on making the coffee herself, which can't be a good thing for the customers.

I hand Kamikaze Driver his coffee and he pays me, giving me a dollar for a tip to make up for the fact he didn't tip me at all on Monday. Then I take a seat behind the elderly lady with the laundry bag who rides this bus every day I do.

When we stop at the railroad crossing because a train is passing by, I hear Kamikaze swear. He hates not making it across before the train. They're long freight trains, and can take five minutes to go by. It messes up his entire life, it seems like, from his reaction.

Seconds later he gets up from his seat and turns around. I try not to make eye contact, but he has removed his sunglasses and is gazing right at me. Then he shuts off the motor and takes the keys. He walks right toward me.

I scrunch down in my seat, trying to avoid him. It's impossible. He puts his hand on the back of my seat. "The coffee is not good today. Not good at all." He tries to hand the cup back to me. "Taste it."

"What?" I say.

"Try this. It's undrinkable. It's lukewarm, it's as weak as a drink at a family wedding on a small budget," he says.

I stare up at him, thinking, I should not have let Jamie make the coffee. Jamie's Java Blend strikes again.

"Come on, taste it," he tells me.

"Are you crazy?" I ask. "I mean, no offense. But you've been sipping out of that cup. I'm not tasting it now," I say.

Kamikaze looks like he's about to explode. His beard is literally twitching. It may always twitch, but I've never been close enough to find out before.

"You know what?" he says, his slightly bloodshot blue eyes unwavering. "Everyone in your generation is so freaked out about germs. When I was your age, I shared everything with everybody."

I get a really icky feeling when he mentions sharing. "Are you talking about free love?" I ask, not wanting to hear his answer. A man in his fifties who insists on wearing a peace button every day frightens me.

"I'm talking about living, about not being afraid of living," he says.

"What makes you think we're afraid of living?" I ask. "That's the stupidest thing I've ever heard. Just because I don't want to catch something—"

"What would you *catch*? I don't have anything," he says. "I'm as much of a healthy, red-blooded American as you are."

I decide to get back to the subject. "Look, if the coffee's that bad, then why would I even *want* to taste it?" I ask him.

He shakes his head. "Forget it. But next time you ride the bus, I want a free coffee," he says. "Tell your manager."

"Look, it was my manager who *made* that awful coffee. And you know, you don't exactly give us perfect rides every day," I point out. "Maybe *I* want a free ride."

"You wouldn't know what to do with a free ride if it hit you in the face," he says. Then he goes back up to the driver's seat, starts the bus, and we roar across the railroad tracks just as the bar lifts. The woman in front of me turns around and pats my arm in sympathy.

When we pull up in front of Edison High, Charlotte is waiting for me at the curb. "Don't get off—I'm getting on," she says when I start down the bus steps.

"What?" I ask.

"We're not going," Charlotte tells me. "I don't know how you say that in French, and I don't care."

Behind me, I hear Kamikaze Driver clearing his throat impatiently.

"But—wait. Why aren't we going?" I ask.

"Because it's a beautiful day, because we only have afternoons to ourselves this summer, and because our teacher hasn't shown up for three weeks," she says.

"But what if today is the day? What if Monsieur LeFleur is finally here—and we're not?" I ask.

"Please move out of the stairwell so that the bus can clear the stop," Kamikaze says. He sounds like he's reading off a bus driver training manual.

"Fleming, wake up. LeFleur's not coming! If by some slim chance it happens . . . then we'll just be *absent*," she says in her bad French accent. "We will bring Monsieur *le sick note* next time. *Oui?*"

We start laughing and Kamikaze Driver gets out of his seat. "You both need to get on the bus *now*, and sit down," he tells us. "People are waiting and I have a schedule to keep."

Charlotte drops her fare into the box. "Lighten up," she says. "This isn't a matter of life or death, is it?"

"How would you know?" Kamikaze says as he glares at her.

"So do you *ever* have a day off?" I ask him as he sits back down. He revs the accelerator and won't even make eye contact with me. Me, his personal coffee wench. Completely ignored. Charlotte and I shuffle to a seat halfway back and are flung together as the bus pulls back into traffic.

"So where are we going?" I ask.

"The mall," Charlotte says, popping her gum as she looks out the window. "If I'm going to do this streaking thing, I'll need a cowboy hat."

I glance over at the woman with the laundry bag, who raises her eyebrow.

I hope Charlotte isn't talking about going to Western Wear Bonanza. I've already been attacked once today. Then I remember how Mr. Stinson might sponsor my dad, how he's giving him all those clothes to skate in. "Um, Charlotte?" I say. "There's something I have to tell you."

And on the way to the mall, I explain about my father's latest skating job. I expect her to laugh so hard that she falls off the seat, which isn't hard to do with Kamikaze at the wheel, but instead she's impressed and says she can't wait to see him skate.

Me? I can wait.

When we walk into the mall, the place is completely deserted. It almost looks closed, except for the seniors who are cruising around the walkway, getting their air-conditioned exercise.

"Man, talk about slow. I was hoping we'd *see* people

here. People under seventy, I mean—I get enough geri-atrics at work. You know, this is so lame. We've got to do something fun this weekend," Charlotte says.

"Like what?" I ask. We pass the two-screen Sunset Cinema and its popcorn smell fills the air for several yards.

"I don't know. That's the problem," Charlotte says. "The only thing I'm looking forward to is streaking at Rodeo Days."

"Well, the only thing *I'm* looking forward to is my mother's water breaking," I tell her.

Charlotte and I both start laughing.

"We're pathetic," I say.

"No, no, no." Charlotte stops to check out a pair of sandals on a spinner that juts out from a store into our path. "*We're* not pathetic. We're fine. We're good. We're fine*good* even," she teases me. "It's this place. It's just so hot and so *slow* here."

"It's like a bus stuck in traffic with broken air-condi-tioning," I say as we continue walking. "That happened last week, on my way home from French class. And—"

"Fleming? You're telling *bus stories*," Charlotte inter-rupts. "Do you see what I'm talking about?"

We both start to laugh again. She's completely right.

"Why don't you and Ray go somewhere, on a trip?" I suggest. If I were with Steve, that's what I'd want to do.

"My mom would not let me do that," she says. "Not in a million years."

"But she'll let you streak?" I ask.

"She won't know about that until it's over," she says. "Anyway, I don't even know if I like Ray all that much—enough to spend a bunch of time in a car with him, I mean. He's sort of boring me. It's like all he ever wants to do is work out."

"Well, he has to keep the arms looking good," I reason as we pass the food court and arrive outside Western Wear Bonanza. "You know," I say before we go in, trying to talk her out of it, "they'll have you arrested if you do it. Lindville's a small town. They'll figure out who you are. You'll never live it down."

"So? Maybe that's a good thing," Charlotte says. "So I get a rep. So what? Knowing my mom, we'll move soon enough, anyway."

"Don't say that! You're not stranding me here—you can't," I say.

"Okay, I'll tell her we're staying." Charlotte smiles. "Now, come on—let's find us some hats."

"Okay, but remember—if you see the owner, be nice," I say. "He's not fond of me."

Charlotte marches into Western Wear Bonanza, squeezing between two large circular racks of turquoise, orange, and red Western-style shirts with contrasting yokes, divided into L–XL and XXL–4X.

I know I shouldn't go in, that Mr. Stinson will go ballistic when he sees me. But if he's willing to outfit my dad for the rodeo, he can't have too many hard feelings toward me. Right? And what am I going to do, not shop for the rest of my Lindville life, just because I don't want to bump into Mr. Stinson? That's ridiculous.

It's terrible logic, but I go into the store, skulking as well as someone five foot eight can skulk. Charlotte's already at the counter, asking to try on the expensive hats behind the glass. I don't recognize the girl working, but I instantly feel sorry for her—not because of Charlotte, but because of her boss.

I stuff a cheap straw hat onto my head for camouflage and meander around the store, keeping an eye on Charlotte and an eye on the back office door. The rawhide chin strap tickles me and the strong smell of leather reminds me of trying to fit boots onto people's feet and how much I loathed it. I take the hat off and stack it on top of some others. Then I stare at the wall of Mr. Stinson's photographs of himself, posing with winning rodeo riders and bulls like Insane Zane.

"Got it!" Charlotte says, running over to me with a white cowboy hat. "It's *perfect*. Check it out." She tries it on with a giant smile on her face. "Isn't it great?"

"It looks good," I say, nodding. Her hair hits her shoulders in a wave. "You look like one of the girls in the saddle club—you could even be voted rodeo queen," I tease her, knowing that the real Lindville rodeo queens, including some girls from our high school, are accomplished riders, that they'd be miles away before I even figured out how to get onto a horse.

Charlotte turns back and forth, admiring herself in front of the mirror. "I prefer 'rodeo princess,' actually. Now if I could only ride a horse." She takes off the hat and hands it to me. "Can you hold on to this for a sec while I try some shirts on?"

"Uh, sure," I say, glancing around the store.

"Be right back." Charlotte grabs a few shirts and blouses on her way into a dressing room, and I follow her, holding her new hat, which I put on. I stand in front of the three-way mirror to see how it looks on me.

Suddenly, behind me in one of the three mirrors, there's Mr. Stinson. His arms are crossed in front of his slightly round stomach.

I look in the mirror at him, not wanting to turn around. It feels like a showdown in an old Western movie.

"Precisely what are *you* doing here, Miss Farrell?" Mr. Stinson demands, lowering his tortoiseshell glasses to get a better look at me.

"Shopping?" I whimper.

He narrows his bushy eyebrows and they meet in a tangled-looking tuft above his nose, like a facial tumbleweed. "Shopping," he repeats.

"Yes," I say, gently taking the cowboy hat off of my head. "My friend wanted a hat."

"Your friend, is that right?" Mr. Stinson stares at the

hat in my hand. "And where is this *friend*?"

"She's in the dressing room," I say meekly.

"Oh, really." Mr. Stinson seems to sort of laugh, as a strange-sounding snort escapes his nose. "This is all just a ruse for you to come in here, isn't it? Are you here to ask for your job back? Fed up with the petrol station? Are you that *daft*, then?"

"No, of course not," I say. "I still work at Gas 'n Git, and she's already bought this hat. And as soon as she tries on some shirts, we'll be out of here."

"Hmm. Yes, you will." Mr. Stinson starts refolding and stacking T-shirts. He doesn't move more than three feet away, as if he's afraid I'll shoplift.

"So," I say, trying to be friendly. "How's business?"

He turns to me and raises an eyebrow.

Wrong question. I decide to try again. "So, my father said you might sponsor him?" I ask.

"We'll see," Mr. Stinson says, the way a parent would.

"He was showing me all the clothes you sent over. That's really great. My dad won't let you down," I say. *Unlike me.* "I mean, he's an incredible skater, a great performer. He's a perfectionist. And he can definitely win over a crowd."

"Well." Mr. Stinson looks surprised that I'm talking so much. "That's very nice, but it all depends on his rodeo show."

"Whose rodeo show?" Charlotte asks, coming out of

the dressing room. She's wearing a white satiny blouse with fringe around its yoke. It's not her usual style, but somehow she pulls it off and looks good in it.

Mr. Stinson turns, and his face lights up as he examines her. "That looks dead gorgeous on you," he says. "May I ask—is it for the rodeo? The parade, perhaps?" He smiles. He's really turning on his retail charm.

"Maybe pre-parade," Charlotte says, and I stifle a laugh.

"It comes in eight colors," Mr. Stinson says. "May I show you the royal blue? It would accent the hat quite nicely." He grabs the white hat from me, and runs off to fetch Charlotte more clothes.

Charlotte looks at me and holds up her hands. "I guess I'm going to look like a rodeo princess whether I want to or not."

I can't believe Mr. Stinson is being so nice to Charlotte. I thought he'd hate her, because she's friends with me. Maybe that means he's starting to forgive me. If he's considering sponsoring my dad, he must be.

Of course, it's only taken him seven months.

Aging Prematurely

It's Friday night and I'm on my way to meet Charlotte at Shady Prairies. Mom's upstairs giving the kids their baths, so I'm off the hook for the evening. I'm halfway out the door at 7:30, in my socks and holding my Rollerblades, when my father suddenly calls out, "P. F., got a second? I need a word with you."

His voice isn't very happy-sounding, so I shut the front door and go stand nervously in the doorway to the kitchen. I hope this isn't about me, in any way—not my visit to Western Wear Bonanza, or the fact I let the kids watch TV all morning instead of playing educational games with them, or about my skipping French. "What's up?"

"Well, it's time to tally up where you are," Dad says. He jumps up and turns down the radio, which is tuned to classic rock, as usual. "Make sure your finances are in order and see where we are, loan-wise."

"Okay, but I'm kind of on my way out," I say. "Could we do this tomorrow?"

"Nope," Dad says.

I sink into a chair across from him and we go over my latest paycheck and what I've already paid him and Mom, and what I still owe them. I write him a check, while he launches into a lecture about financial responsibility, about how as soon as I pay them back, I need to start putting away money in a savings account so I can save up for a car of my own, if I'm serious about taking a trip. He whips out his calculator and starts calculating car-loan rates for me, the way he's always doing for clients and their mortgages. "The thing about amortization is . . ." he says.

I tune out and start daydreaming about the trip. I see myself in a convertible, cruising along that California highway by the Pacific Ocean, the one that's in all the TV commercials and movies. I go north from there and have to put up the top, because I'm in Oregon and it's raining. I head farther north to Seattle, where I stop for coffee, because coffee is very big there and because I'm tired from driving. I go north to Vancouver, and there's a ferry leaving for Victoria, so there I am, on the deck, drinking my Seattle coffee, which has sort of gone cold—

But wait. I can't do all that by myself.

Before I take off in my convertible, I pick up Steve, who gets out of work from IHOP. I pull up in the parking lot and Jacqui is clinging to his apron and not wanting him to leave with me, so he takes off the apron and leaves her clutching it, drying her tears on it, as he tosses a beat-up old leather suitcase into the trunk and—

"P. F., are you listening?"

I clear my throat and sit up straighter in my chair. "Of course, Dad. Of course I am. And I appreciate all this advice, I really do. I should get going, though." I stand up, get my backpack, and grab my keys off the hook by the door.

Dad purses his lips and looks very disappointed in me. First I gave up skating; now I'm giving up liking math. "P. F., do me a favor," he says as he gets up from the kitchen table. "Take this a little more seriously. You've made a dent, but you still owe this family more than five hundred dollars." His voice is as cold as the outdoor ice rink in January.

"I know, Dad," I say. "That's why we have a payment plan."

"Which you're falling behind on," he says. "I'm expecting big things from you this summer, P. F. Good things. Please don't disappoint me."

He turns off the radio and leaves the kitchen, and a few seconds later I hear him put classical music on the CD player. He must be choosing music for his program again. He hasn't been happy with the last eight pieces he's tried to choreograph to. He keeps skipping from one track to another. He's not happy right now. When he's not happy, his skating suffers.

I can't picture classical music at the rodeo, where country and western is usually blaring from overhead speakers. Then again, I can't picture an ice rink, or a skating cowboy. Or maybe I just don't want to.

The sun is still out when I skate up in front of Shady Prairies. Charlotte's waiting for me in the lobby. "How was work?" I ask her.

"Easy," she says. "Except for the fact that everyone ordered liver and onions, and we ran out and I had to convince the second seating that chipped beef was just as good. Which nobody believed. And they were right. So a bunch of people started talking about how they need a new dining director here, and how there wasn't enough wheat bread at breakfast for toast."

"Mm-hmm," I say. "Very interesting." I take off my Rollerblades and slip them into my backpack, then put on my black rubber flip-flops.

Charlotte starts laughing. "Sorry. I guess I just needed to vent. So, are you ready for an adventure?"

"That depends. What is it, and does it involve eating chipped beef? Whatever that is."

"*No.* We're going for a little ride," she whispers to me as we leave the lobby.

"In what?" I ask. "Is Ray coming? I mean, is he already here?"

"Forget Ray," she says. "We sort of broke up last night."

"You *did*? What happened?" I ask.

"It's not important. I mean, it was just a dumb fight, but the point is that we don't need Ray. We've got our own wheels."

"You got your Mom's car again? Wow, has it been a month already?" I ask.

"No, I actually don't have a car. But we are sort of renting one tonight," Charlotte whispers. "Free of charge. Come on."

I figure she's talking about someone lending her a car. I can't imagine that she's talked one of the retired Shady residents into lending her their Cadillac, but maybe she has. I've learned not to doubt Charlotte. She makes things happen. She insists on it.

We walk through an employee parking lot off to the side of the main building as the sun slowly sinks on the horizon. "See those carts over there?" she asks.

"The golf carts?" I look at the two small beige vehicles with the initials SP written in green script on the roof—as if they need to be identifiable by helicopter, like big-city buses.

"Yeah. But they're not used for golf. They're for carrying guests and visitors around, to show them the place. And for delivering packages and helping people with groceries and luggage and stuff." Charlotte rubs her hands together. "And tonight, one of them is going to carry *us* to the Lot."

169

"We're going to steal a golf cart?" I ask, feeling a little skeptical about this plan.

"Don't worry, we steal them all the time. Well, not steal exactly. Sometimes the guys from the grounds crew tool around on them, so we hitch rides and cruise around the property. Like before dinner starts, after we're all set up. They're really fun." She takes a key chain out of her pocket and shakes it in my face. "And I've got a key, so it's not technically stealing at all."

"How did you get that?" I ask.

"It's a long story. Don't worry about it."

"Won't we be sort of obvious?"

"We'll take the back roads," she says, popping her gum. "And it's nighttime. And if anyone asks how we got this, or what we're doing . . ."

I wait for her to finish the sentence. She doesn't.

"Then what?" I ask.

"I figured out how we're getting to the Lot. *You* figure out what to say if we get caught."

I think about this for a second. I really shouldn't do this. I know that. If the police are around tonight and we get caught, it might be decades before I get my license back from my parents. I could be carless for the rest of my life. And that's just the tip of the crimeberg.

Then again, it *is* Friday night, and what else are we going to do?

"Okay," I say. "But you're driving."

An hour later, we are bouncing down Twelfth Street in a golf cart. Its shocks are completely gone, and I think I have about three bugs in my teeth, not to mention one dead gnat in my right eye. I understand more than ever the purpose of windshields. Everyone's cruising tonight, so we pull out from a side street and fall into formation, safely sandwiched between a Jeep and an SUV.

"It's like being on a float!" Charlotte says, waving at anyone and everyone, people passing us, people driving in the other direction.

It's my job to wave and also to study the crowd for cops. Everyone is staring at us and pointing. I didn't think we could get away with this. It's impossible.

But we are getting away with it. We made it here, and everyone's seen us. The police must be busy somewhere else. This is my first lucky break in a while, so I'm going to enjoy it. I see friends from Edison and wave at them. I see Steve and Jacqui parked in the Lot and wave to them. Steve waves back, his face lighting up when he sees us. He walks closer to the street to get a better look, while Jacqui just looks confused.

What's really bizarre is that I don't really care about them right now—about whether they're together, or whether Steve notices how much fun I'm having without him. I don't really care about anything right now. I feel like anything is possible tonight.

I see some people from our French class and we wave to them. "If Monsieur LeFleur could see us now . . . what would he think?" I ask Charlotte. "Well, who cares what he'd think? Because he doesn't exist!" I declare.

Mike and Ray pass us in Ray's pickup. Mike leans out of the passenger-side window and yells, "What are you guys doing? Where did you get that thing?"

"Charlotte! They'll fire you!" Ray screams across the seat at us.

"Who cares?" she calls back. Then she swears and says to me, "I forgot, I'm not *talking* to him."

We start laughing, and a few blocks later Charlotte suddenly takes a right turn, pulling into Dale's Fifties Drive-Up, where waiters and waitresses deliver the food to your car by skating on old-fashioned roller skates.

"Should we really do this?" I ask Charlotte. Now that we're out of the clump of cars, I feel even *more* conspicuous.

She pulls around to the darkest, most secluded parking place in the back, where people go to make out. Nobody's back here but us, which is a relief. "I'm buying," Charlotte offers, and she lifts the little red phone beside the cart to place our order, a fry basket and chocolate shakes.

"I figured we should stop," she says afterward. "I don't want to run out of gas, or battery power or whatever this thing runs on. Anyway, we made our point, didn't we?"

"Um . . . what was our point?" I ask.

"I don't know!" she says, laughing.

"Me neither, but it was a good one. People were freaking out," I say. "I'm surprised we didn't cause an accident, especially with my track record. It's amazing, actually." Then again, I wasn't driving, was I?

The waitress comes out to deliver our order a few minutes later. It's so dark where we're parked that she doesn't notice a clump of onion rings someone must have dropped earlier, and she trips and crashes to the pavement.

Somehow she manages to skillfully hold our tray in the air without spilling anything. It's as if this has happened to her before. She stands up and dusts herself off, brushing a large onion ring off her bare leg.

"Are you all right?" Charlotte and I call over to her.

"Fine—just give me a minute," she replies.

"Fleming, you should be the one who works here; it's so obvious," Charlotte says. "You skate a lot better than she does. You're fast—you'd get good tips."

"I know." I sigh. "That's what I told my parents. But they refused to let me wear the uniform."

"It *is* a bit short," Charlotte says as the waitress approaches in a modified fifties-style skirt that barely covers her rear end. She looks like she's my mother's age, so it seems extra risqué.

When she gets closer, she looks at us suspiciously as she tries to figure out where she can attach the tray. "Where did you get this thing?" she asks. "Are you supposed to be driving this around at night—on the streets?"

Charlotte turns to me and smiles. "Fleming?"

"Oh. Well, see, this is part of a new teen outreach program at Shady Prairies," I say. "They're trying to sponsor a couple of teens every summer, and give them new opportunities. They chose me and Charlotte this summer."

The waitress looks me in the eye as she sets the tray on the hood of the cart. "And how does the cart fit in?"

"They think we should experience life slowly at first," I say. "You know, like the expression 'looking at the world through rose-colored glasses'? They want us to look at the world going like fifteen miles per hour. So that we can absorb it all, drink it all in. So we don't get ahead of ourselves and go too fast. This is, like, their whole point—to protect us from aging prematurely."

The waitress studies my face for a few seconds. My heart is beating so fast that it must show through my T-shirt, like something out of an old Bugs Bunny cartoon. Beside me, Charlotte has stopped, mid inserting straw into chocolate shake. The whole world is on pause while we wait for a not very coordinated roller skater to tell us our fate.

Then she nods. "You know my mother lives out there. I bet she'd like to get involved in the program. I'll have to mention it to her." She takes our money and skates back to the restaurant.

"Oh, God," Charlotte says.

"What?" I ask.

"That was so scary."

"I know," I say. "I thought for sure she was going to bust us."

"No—not that. I mean the way you just came up with that story," she says.

"I had a lot of time to think it up," I tell her. "We were going like ten miles an hour, remember?"

"So we could live more slowly," Charlotte says, paraphrasing me. "Oh, yeah. *That's* what we want to do."

I Am Sunshine

All weekend I sit around knowing that I've gotten away with something. My father's so wrapped up in selling houses and preparing for his rodeo performance that he doesn't even have time to notice that I look guilty. I like having this secret that nobody knows about, and my parents don't know why I'm in such a good mood or why I volunteer to baby-sit for two hours while they go grocery shopping. It's all because of the golf cart.

At work on Saturday night, I give random customers coupons for free specialty drinks and free muffins.

Charlotte drops by to visit me and drinks three vanilla lattes in an hour. When I introduce her to Denny, she says, "Did Fleming tell you what we did last night?"

"No," he says slowly, glancing at me. "Wait, don't tell me. Baby-sitting again?"

"No. We drove a golf cart through town," Charlotte says.

Denny laughs, and seems instantaneously smitten with her. "No, really?"

"Really," Charlotte says.

"Well, that's nothing compared to some of the stuff Fleming's done before," Denny says. "Like how she smashed the window at the mall by propelling Santa into it—did she tell you about that?"

They keep joking around about me and my bad job experiences. I laugh, too. It *is* funny. And I can see that Denny is really into Charlotte. After she leaves, I don't even tease him about it. Maybe she's into him, too. Maybe Ray is out of the picture for good, and Denny is now in the picture. Who knows? Ever since Friday night I feel like anything is possible.

My father comes to pick me up at 11:20, late as usual, but I don't point this out. Instead we talk about his new program on the way home. When we get there, I listen to the different musical numbers he's considering and tell him none of them will work, but not in a negative way. I run upstairs, get all my CDs, and stay up until 2:00 A.M. trying to create a medley using his music and mine, combining his favorites from the Rolling Stones, Aerosmith, and the Beatles with the Foo Fighters, Lenny Kravitz, and Beck.

When he looks uneasy Sunday morning as I play the music for him, and tells me the rodeo organizers are pushing for something country—in fact insisting on it—I don't take it personally. I tell him we'll keep working on it and remind him that Elvis Stojko used nontraditional music and still scored 6.0s. Dad starts smiling and reminiscing about Elvis Stojko, for a second forgetting he's not shooting for a world championship here.

My name is not P. F. Farrell anymore.

My name is definitely not Peggy.

I am Sunshine.

Sunday afternoon, after Lamaze class—during which I am so kind and helpful that even Monica takes notice and tells the other birth coaches to watch *me*, of all people— Mom tells me in the elevator that we need to pick up party supplies for the twins' birthday on the way home, and then when we get home, that she and Dad are leaving for a friend's barbecue, so I'll need to watch the kids.

All this information doesn't even bother me; I just absorb it like a thirsty paper towel and keep walking in the direction of the minivan.

We stop at Party Party Party, and as we walk in, I wonder whether Torvill started saying everything three times after a trip here. We have fifteen minutes to fill a cart with birthday decorations, and we're on a budget. I summon my math skills and pick out cups, plates, hats, balloons, and party favors. All of them match the twins' theme: Five.

Or, according to Torvill, "five, five, five."

"Peggy, you're good at this." My mother compliments me on the drive home. "You can buy all the party decorations from now on."

I think, *As if I wasn't going to be doing that, anyway*, but I don't say that. I just say, "Thanks." That's how good my mood is.

When Mom turns onto our street, she suddenly winces and reaches for her belly. "Oh. Wow. That was a strong one."

"A kick?" I ask.

She shakes her head. "A contraction."

"What? You're going into labor? But you're not ready. I'm not ready—"

"Relax, Peggy. It's nothing like that," she says as she pulls into the driveway. "I'm not in labor. However, I do think I should go inside and lie down for a while, because I'm feeling uncomfortable." She calmly puts the car in park.

"Maybe the baby doesn't like shopping," I say as I help Mom out of the car. Then I see a strange figure sitting on our front steps. It's wearing a black leather vest over a white T-shirt, and jeans, despite the fact that the afternoon heat is intolerable. What is *Denny* doing at my house?

"Wait a minute." Mom's eyes narrow as she spots him, too. "Who's that?"

"He's the guy I work with at Gas 'n Git," I tell her. "I have no idea what he's doing here, but that's who he is."

"Oh. Well, all right." I quickly introduce Denny to Mom, and then she goes inside to lie down. She's not feeling well enough to interrogate him.

"So what are you doing here?" I ask Denny as I get the shopping bags out of the car. "Why are you waiting outside?"

"Your dad said the kids were taking a nap, so." Denny shrugs. "Anyway, could you give this to Charlotte? I thought you'd see her before I do, so . . ." He hands me a brown paper bag.

"That depends. What is it?" I ask.

"I made her a tape," he says. "Of my favorite U2 songs. We were talking about it and she said she sort of liked them, but she didn't have any CDs, so . . . you know. If I had a CD burner, these would be CDs, but I can't afford one because I'm saving all my money for a trip to Ireland, so they're not."

I am so jealous that for a second I can't speak. Everyone has plans to get out of Lindville. "You're going to Ireland?" I ask. *"When?"*

"I don't know. Soon, though," he says.

I try not to hate him. "This feels heavier than just one tape." I shake the bag and hear rattling cassette cases inside.

"Yeah. Well, it was going to be one ninety-minute tape," he says. Where his little mustache used to be, there's now a red strip of skin that looks like sunburn. "But then

I couldn't fit them all on there, so . . . it's actually three and a half tapes worth of songs."

I don't say anything for a minute, because I'm thinking how Charlotte has three hundred minutes of U2 and how nice it would be to have someone that devoted to either me or to my band.

Thwarted

Inside Edison High the next day, everything is as usual. We have the golf player substitute again. "Unfortunately, Monsieur LeFleur has suffered a relapse in his health, due to the stress of attending the family funeral," the sub tells us.

"What? But the funeral was two weeks ago," I say. "And last week he wasn't here because of a family emergency."

"Yes. Well, I'm not sure exactly what's going on, but he won't be able to make it today. However, he wanted me to thank you all very much for your cards, and I have corrected homework to hand back to you, and a worksheet, as well as a tape of him teaching a class, which we can all listen to."

"Someone else's class?" I ask. "Like, we're getting a repeat?"

"Are we going to get credit for this course? Because I'm really starting to wonder here," Charlotte says.

"You will certainly get credit—if you can pass the exam at the end of the summer term," the substitute says. "It's an oral and written exam."

"How are we supposed to pass an exam when we never speak French in here?" another student asks. "There aren't enough subs that speak French, and we never practice. It's not fair."

"I'm sure Monsieur LeFleur will go easy on you. He's not expecting you to make a hole in one without a lesson from the pro, if you catch my drift," she says.

We don't. Or at least I don't want to. If I start having a rapport with golf pros, I'm not sure what that would mean about me, but it can't be good.

"As usual, he has prepared special materials for you." She walks around the classroom, her golf-shoe spikes clicking on the linoleum floor.

I stare at the worksheet she places on my desk. Monsieur LeFleur has made a list of vocabulary words for us, and we have to use them in French sentences. This is the list, which is titled Emotions:

Sad
Gloomy
Cheerless
Angry
Furious
Irate

Enraged
Depressed
Frustrated
Disturbed
Thwarted
Despondent
Hopeless

I'm not sure why the last word isn't *suicidal*, because it seems like the most natural progression. I go up to the front of the classroom, where the golfer is sitting at the desk filling out an attendance sheet, or her scorecard, perhaps. "Listen," I whisper to her. "Is Monsieur LeFleur dying? Does he have inoperable cancer or something?"

"What? No. That's absurd. Do you realize how absurd that is?" she asks me.

I nod. "Yes. But look at this list. The man is in trouble somehow."

"Well, he's not that sick," she says.

"Not *that* sick? Then how sick is he?" I ask.

"That's personal—but he's not dying. And I really have no idea. I'm sure it's just a sort of flu," she says.

I put my hands on my hips. "Then explain where he's been for the past three and a half weeks. The most dedicated teacher in Lindville. Missing."

She shrugs. "Look, I don't know; they don't tell me any more than you. All I know is, he has someone pick up the students' work and drop off his assignments. But I think you should go back to your seat now and get to work on that . . . worksheet."

I glare at her for a minute, then go back to my seat.

Charlotte taps my arm with her pen. "You were sort of harassing her up there. What happened?"

"I'm so mad about this class. I just—" I stare at the worksheet. "I really identify with this list right now."

"Me too," Charlotte says. "Except—what does *thwarted* mean?"

"You know. Me and Steve. Because of Jacqui," I explain. "Like that."

"So why didn't he just write *sucky*?" Charlotte asks.

"I don't think sucky is a word," I say. "But it should be." In French it could be *sucké*, and I could use it in several sentences, all relating to this summer.

We both focus on the list for a few minutes. Then Charlotte leans over and asks, "Hey, you want to go to IHOP after class?"

"Sure," I say. Then I remember: I have to take the kids to the park. Maybe this is a good thing. I'm not sure if I could take watching the "IHOPpers in Love" routine again. "Actually, I can't. But hold on—I have something for you." I dig the paper bag of cassettes out of my bag and hand it to her. "These are for you. From Denny. His U2 favorites."

Charlotte peers into the bag. "Wow. This is so cool!"

"He'll probably quiz you sometime, so just be prepared, okay?" I ask.

Suddenly Monsieur LeFleur's voice booms out of the tape player on the sub's desk and she jumps up to turn down the volume. "Sorry, kids!" she says as a man's voice screams, *"Bonjour, mes amis!"*

Wild Streak

I finish loading the dishwasher as fast as I can on Tuesday night.

"Peggy, don't break the dishes," Mom says critically, as she sits at the kitchen table, watching me. "Just put them in."

"Mom, don't call me Peggy," I say. "All right?" I drop forks and spoons into the silverware basket.

"Well, *you're* touchy," Mom says, which is a funny comment coming from someone who's so cranky she swore at the stove earlier for burning the kids' mac and cheese.

"Ray and Charlotte are picking me up in two minutes," I say. They're back together again, so I have a ride tonight. I wash the saucepans and drop them into the drainer, while Mom goes into the living room to monitor Dean and Torvill, who are building a fort out of the sofa pillows.

"You're going out with Charlotte *again*?" my father asks as he holds Dorothy in the air above his head, preparing her for her career as either an air force pilot or a pairs skater doing a lift. "It's a Tuesday night."

"Dad, I'm not on a school schedule."

"I know. It's just that you work at the store tomorrow morning. You've got French. And I'm not exactly sure how I feel about you spending so much time with Charlotte."

"What do you mean by that?" I ask. "Don't you like her?"

"Sure. Of course. But she has quite a wild streak, doesn't she?" Dad says. "I could tell, when I met her outside French class that day. She just has that look. Or maybe it's an *attitude*."

"Wild streak? No, not really," I say, thinking, *Unless she really does streak*. "I mean, she's creative. She has a lot of creative energy." And creative ideas about driving nontraditional vehicles on town streets. But that hasn't gotten back to my parents yet, so I don't think it's going to.

"Translation: wild streak," my father says as he twirls Dorothy upside down. "P. F., I wasn't born yesterday, okay? I had friends like that. I was sort of like that."

I wipe my hands on the dishtowel. "You? Come on, Dad. Be serious."

My father glances at me with a wounded expression. "Why is that so hard to believe?"

"Because!" I peer out the window over the sink to see if Ray and Charlotte are here yet. "You've told me a thousand times how you got up at four to skate before school and how your schedule was so grueling and all that." And I can't exactly picture the male-figure-skating clique being known for its wildness.

"That doesn't mean I didn't occasionally do stupid things," my father says. "So. What do you two *do* exactly, when you go out?"

"Nothing, really. I mean, just hang out with people." I shrug.

"By people, I assume you mean . . . boys?" my father asks. "Anyone in particular I should know about?"

Fortunately, I see Ray's truck pull up outside just then, so I grab my Rollerblade bag just in case I need to skate home later. "I'll be home by eleven," I say.

"Be careful!" my father calls to me. "Don't do anything I wouldn't do."

Two hours later I am making out with Mike Kyle in a do-it-yourself car wash.

I don't know how this happened, but it did. We met up with him at the Lot. Mike wouldn't stop talking about how cool I looked when he saw me skating across town the other day while he was out delivering pizzas in his Geo. He says I should audition for some kind of roller demolition derby they're supposed to be having at

Rodeo Days this year.

"I think there's a roller-skating exhibition for kids, and a demolition derby for cars," I told him. "It's not combined."

"Oh. Well, have you seen *Rollerball*? You could do that. You'd pulverize the competition."

So he thinks of me as a bruiser, I thought. Not exactly the sort of girl anyone wants to go out with. It wasn't exactly shaping up to be a date night, which was fine, because I really didn't feel like yet another gruesome foursome evening, spent staring at Steve—and Jacqui.

I sat on the tailgate of Ray's truck while Mike tried on my Rollerblades. Everyone said they would be too small for him, but the skates fit Mike exactly. He'd never been on Rollerblades before, so I offered to help him out. We went to a corner of the Lot and he held on to my arm as he tried to steady himself. We kept laughing because whenever he got going too fast he'd sort of panic and I had to jog over and keep him from falling. There were all these pieces of broken glass he had to step over.

All of a sudden we heard shouting, and looked back over toward the pickup. "They're just tapes!" Charlotte was screaming. "If you're so mad, then take me home!" She got in and slammed the door. Ray slammed the door, too, and they took off.

"My shoes were in that truck," Mike said, and we started laughing.

So I drove Mike's car, because he was still wearing my skates. I didn't tell him my parents keep my license in a locked box so I can't drive. I figured I wouldn't get pulled over on the way to the Cone Zone, for ice cream.

Afterward he wanted to take me home, and he was driving in his bare feet. It was sort of sexy, because he has really nice toes, which is a very weird thing to notice about a guy when you are hung up on that guy's best friend.

All of a sudden Mike pulled into the car wash. I knew this was a place people went to make out because it's on a side street, and because it's private since it has walls on two sides. But it didn't feel very private to me. There were other couples and cars in the next few bays, and people kept cruising by to see who was there.

Not sure what else to do, I got out of the car, and Mike did, too. I was joking around with the foaming brush and pretending to scrub the rust off Mike's car, which is practically all rust, when Mike just took my arms and sort of gently pushed me back a little toward the concrete wall. He was about my height in his bare feet, and his lips were soft and matched up with mine perfectly, like they were the matching half of a puzzle piece. I knew I was getting carried away, thinking things like this, and I just sort of gave in to it. There was cold water dripping from the rinse wand onto my feet and it was so cool and oasislike. I didn't even care that it smelled like wet metal and bad cleaning agents. Lindville seemed about a million miles away.

"So." Mike smoothes my cheek with his thumb, then kisses me again.

"Wait. Wait!" I push him away. "We shouldn't be doing this," I say. I stare at this yellow caution sign on the wall that shows a person falling down. WARNING: ICE MAY FORM ON WET SURFACES DURING COLD WEATHER.

"Why not?" He lifts a strand of hair off my forehead and starts kissing me again.

I should protest again, a little more forcefully, but I don't. Kissing Mike isn't like kissing Steve, but it's better than nothing. It feels good to be kissed, to have someone want to kiss me.

I shouldn't be doing this, though, because I still want Mike to be Steve. I've spent months obsessing about him. I can't just drop my Steve fantasy in a car wash because of someone's nice toes. Really, really nice toes. And lips.

"I—I should go," I say as I pull away. "I have this really strict curfew, so . . ."

"So we'll just start earlier tomorrow night," he says.

"Right. Exactly. That's exactly what I was thinking," I lie.

I'm jamming my feet into my Rollerblades and telling Mike how I'm going to skate home instead of catching a ride with him, when this single bright headlight shines right on me, like a police flashlight. Then I hear an engine cut off, and the light goes out.

My eyes adjust to the dark again and I see Denny sitting on his motorcycle. He flips up the visor of his helmet and glares at me, as if I've just set fire to a stack of U2 CDs. "What are you doing here?" he asks, making this not-so-sly head gesture toward Mike, who's standing by his car. "People only come here for one thing."

"In that case, what are you doing here? Unless your date fell off the back of your bike and you didn't notice?" I reply. "Or did you plan on washing your motorcycle?"

He leans back on his bike. "For your information, I was sort of looking around," he says. "I thought maybe Charlotte would be around here somewhere. You said you guys were planning to hang around at the Lot tonight, so when you weren't there, I thought I'd drive around and look. So, is she around?"

I shook my head. "She left."

"Where did she go?"

I shrug.

"Did you give her the tapes?" he asks.

"Yes," I say.

"Miss Talkative strikes again," Denny says in disgust, as if I'm deliberately withholding information. Which I am.

Mike pulls out of the car wash, giving me a little wave over his shoulder. He honks the horn a couple of times, then peels out.

"I can't believe you were here with *him*," Denny says

disparagingly. "That's the guy who came into the store, talking about trading in his Camaro. Right?"

"Did you come here just to ruin my night?" I ask.

"Why? Was it really *special*?" Denny asks.

I glare at him. "At least I'm not driving around aimlessly looking for someone. You know, you could always go work at Shady Prairies so you can be close to her," I say. "Jamie would miss you at Gas 'n Git, but she'd get over it."

"Hey, you couldn't even hold a job before you came to Gas 'n Git," Denny scoffs as he starts up his motor again. "And at least I'M not making out with an IDIOT in a CAR WASH!" Denny flips down his visor, revs the engine, and then turns out onto the street. He pulls away from me, going faster and faster, until he has to stop for a red light about two blocks away, which sort of ruins his dramatic exit.

I sit down on the pavement to finish fastening my skates. It wasn't such a horrible thing being with Mike, no matter what Denny said. So he likes me. So . . . okay, good. Someone should.

Suddenly there's a loud sound approaching. I look up and see Denny circling back. He pulls up beside me. "So do you want a ride? Because it's not safe, skating after dark. By yourself."

"No, thanks," I say, getting to my feet.

"Come on." He scoots forward on his seat. "Fleming,

come on. I'm not leaving here without you."

I consider my options. Neither one is all that great. "Do you have an extra helmet?" I ask.

He pulls one out of the black leather bag on the back of the bike. I put it on and climb on behind him. I'm trying to hang on by touching him as little as possible. I start to give him directions, but he reminds me he already knows where I live. I've never ridden on a motorcycle before. I like the way Denny leans the motorcycle down toward the street when he turns corners. It reminds me of the death spiral in pairs skating, where the woman's entire body skims just above the ice.

We're about four blocks from my house when I see the Doberman leap the fence and race toward us.

I'm convinced the dog has some sixth sense that screams "Rollerblade Girl" whenever I'm within leaping range. He sprints out toward the bike, but we blow past him, leaving him stunned and gazing forlornly after us.

Denny drops me off at the end of the block. He must know my parents wouldn't want me showing up on his motorcycle.

"That was the Doberman," I say as I hand him the helmet.

He nods. "I figured."

"So thanks a lot for the ride," I tell him. "And just so you know, Charlotte left tonight because she got into a fight with the guy she's been seeing. A fight over your tapes. Okay?"

"Really?" Denny smiles.

"See you tomorrow morning," I say.

"Yeah, okay. Be careful, Fleming."

"It's only a block."

"All right, don't be careful then," he says. He pushes off with his feet and takes off down the street.

When I walk into the house, my father's sitting at the kitchen table with a sketch pad. There are wavy lines all over the paper, and little figures shaped like animals—or people, I can't tell. "Hey, Dad."

"P. F. You scared me half to death," he says when I speak, catching him off guard.

If you only knew what I did tonight, I think. *You'd be really scared.* "What are you drawing?" I ask. "Your new long program?"

"Um, no," he says, covering the sketch pad with his right hand. "It's my short program. Very short. For the rodeo."

"I thought you were finished with that," I say.

He shakes his head. "I met with the rodeo people tonight. And Mr. Stinson. I did my program for them."

"Did they love it?" I ask.

"Not exactly. They told me I need to make some changes."

"Oh. Well, do you think it'll be okay?"

He chews his thumbnail. "Sure. Of course. It's going to be great." Then he puts his head on the table, doing a face plant on the sketch pad. "Who am I trying to kid? P. F., it's awful. It's going to be the worst program in the history of figure skating." He sits up, and I notice dark circles under his eyes. "I haven't told you this yet, but it has to have an *animal* theme. Sheep, cattle, horses—the things that draw people to the rodeo," he says. "P. F., I don't know a thing about handling livestock. How am I going to do this? Costumes are one thing, but since when do actual *animals* factor into figure skating? They want animals on the ice with me."

I stare at him. I don't want to say anything, but isn't this sort of his problem? He's the one who agreed to skate at a rodeo. I warned him not to.

"I can't even broach the subject with Ludmila. She'd have my head on a platter. I've called a couple of skating friends, and they all think I'm crazy to even attempt this. I still can't think of the right music. Tchaikovsky didn't write about bucking broncos much." He is still scowling as he starts laughing in despair. "Why did I say I'd do this? Am I insane?"

Yes, I think. But he has so much invested in this that I can't say that. "Is it too late to say you're not going to do it?" I ask.

He nods. "Way too late. They've already booked me for three shows a night, starting on the tenth—opening night. I've signed a contract. They've even advanced me some money."

"Oh. Three a night? Really?" That seems like a lot. "Okay. So we'll figure it out," I tell him. "You need a song with animals . . . is that what you said?"

"Yes, but not 'Old McDonald,'" he says. "Something sophisticated. Something I won't be embarrassed to skate to."

I decide not to point out that the entire fact he's skating with livestock is going to be embarrassing enough. "Hey, I'll ask Denny tomorrow," I say. "He knows a lot about music."

My father frowns. "Okay, but I don't want any heavy metal. Make a note of that."

"Don't worry, that's not what he likes."

I'm about to leave the room, when my father says, "So what did you and Charlotte do tonight?"

"Oh, um, not much," I say. "Nothing, really."

"Uh-huh. Well, you're only half an hour late, so that's an improvement, I guess." He taps his pencil against the table, then runs his hand through his thinning hair.

I quietly go upstairs to my room and close the door behind me. I stand at my dresser and look at myself in the mirror. My hair's slightly flattened from the motorcycle helmet, and my cheeks are extra pink. I can't believe my dad didn't notice that.

I also can't believe I was making out with Mike. What

was I thinking? He's the wrong guy. And if he tells Steve about it, would that be a good thing or a bad thing?

I can't figure it out, but I stare at myself in the mirror, wondering what I'm up to.

No French Connection

"This is so easy. You really couldn't think of this yourself?" Denny says the next morning at Gas 'n Git after pressing me for more details on Charlotte, and Ray, and Charlotte's fight with Ray.

"No." I take a gulp of coffee. I cannot wake up this morning.

"He has to skate around a horse and some goats, right?"

"Sheep," I say, sipping.

"Whatever. Okay, are you ready? Here's the song. 'Who's Gonna Ride Your Wild Horses'! U2!" Denny says, as if it's a battle cry. "From *Achtung Baby*."

I try to think of the song. I'm not sure I know it. I'm not sure that I'm convinced. "Is that about horses?" I ask.

"No, but who cares?" Denny says. "That's one of my favorite songs in the entire world."

It's by U2, so doesn't that go without saying? I think.

"And it could work for skating, definitely," he goes on.

"Well, what about . . . a U2 medley or something?" I ask.

Denny looks deathly offended. "U2 doesn't *do* medleys."

"I know that!" I say, irritated and tired of this. "But see—figure skating? It kind of does."

"Hmm." Denny's face is turning a little splotchy. He looks like he's breaking out into a sweat. "If you could forget the animal theme . . ." He starts laughing nervously. "You could use 'Elevation,' that'd be good for skating. Or 'I Fall Down' from *October*—for all the jumps and stuff?" He continues to laugh nervously. "How about 'So Cruel,' you know, he could make it into this sort of statement about cruelty to animals. How about 'Even Better than the Real Thing' or 'With or Without You'? Or wait—he could forget the animals, do a lemon theme and use 'Lemon,' because that has that sort of clubby sound skaters go for." He's gone crazy. He's babbling. I wonder if I should slap him to stop him from reciting song names.

"A *lemon* theme?" I ask as the automatic door sensor rings. I turn and see Charlotte walking into the store. So that's why Denny is suddenly acting so weird.

Her face lights up and she hurries up to me. "I thought you were working today, but I couldn't remember—I took a chance and caught the bus. So Kamikaze says he wants a triple mocha today with extra whipped cream instead of his usual."

"Really?" I ask.

"No, I'm just kidding. *God*, can you imagine him and whipped cream and his beard?" She shudders and looks at Denny. "Hey. Thanks for the tapes."

Denny clears his throat and says, "Hey, no problem," then rushes off to pour himself a soda from the fountain. He stares at Charlotte while he's filling his cup with ice, and the crushed ice cascades onto the floor. He's just so suave.

While he cleans up, I tell Charlotte what happened the night before with Mike, after she and Ray left us in the Lot.

"You kissed Mike! Like, a lot," Charlotte concludes.

"Not that much."

"No, I can tell." She stares at me. "So how was it?"

"Weirdnice," I tell her, flustered by remembering very vividly how it felt. It wasn't like Steve. But was it worse? Or better? "I just don't think I'd want to go out with him. As anything long-term."

"Oh, is that all? Who cares about *that*?" Charlotte asks.

I laugh. "Denny actually showed up," I whisper to her, "looking for you. Then he gave me a hard time about being with Mike. Then he gave me a ride home."

"I think he likes *you*, not me," she says.

I shake my head. "No. Really. You're the one. I didn't even get one tape," I tell her.

"Hmm. I'll have to think about this," she says. She

202

looks over at Denny as he gets back behind the counter to ring up customers' sales.

I hurry over to a customer who's waiting for coffee. As I make her a latte, Charlotte comes behind the counter and says, "So you're coming to meet me at work tomorrow for the fireworks, right? We'll go see them together?"

"Sure," I say, "but what happened with Ray last night?"

"Forget Ray," she says in a low voice. "It's over. *Really* over this time."

I look over at Denny. Maybe there is hope for him.

Charlotte picks out a banana-nut muffin for breakfast, and I pour her a cup of coffee. She grabs a *Lindville Gazette*, takes her coffee, and sits at one of the tiny tables we have by the windows.

"Look at this!" she cries a minute later. She gets up from the table and comes over to me and Denny. "That robber guy is hitting the next town now. He held up a *grocery* store. Aren't you guys scared?" she asks.

Denny jiggles a key in the register. "Nah. Not really." He seems to have recovered a little from his first glimpse of Charlotte.

"God. Who wants to come to work thinking someone's going to stick a gun in their face? You guys are crazy to work here."

Denny giggles, and then must realize he sounds funny doing that, because he stops. He coughs, then says in a lower voice, "Yeah, it's just something you sort of deal with in this job. But it's a good place to work. We don't get harassed."

"Much," I add as I see Coffee Breath's car pull up in front. He's here for his second Tanker of the day.

"You guys are brave," Charlotte says. Then she goes back and sits at her table by the window.

"She has no idea," I say to Denny, but he's too busy staring at Charlotte. I know he wants to go sit with her and talk to her and ask about the tapes—and tell her about the songs he's writing. But he doesn't. He shows remarkable restraint. He doesn't even flirt with me to make her jealous. He's . . . mature or something.

Or else his Bono obsession doesn't leave room for anyone else in his heart. If Bono ever came in here, I don't want to think how Denny might act.

After I get out of work, Charlotte and I take the bus over to Edison for French class.

Kamikaze half grunts when I hand him his usual coffee with cream. He gives me back one of the dollars I hand him, as a tip, but he doesn't say a word.

"Good afternoon to you, too!" Charlotte says as she shows him her transfer.

He looks up at her, and then over at me. "Don't tell me. The mall again?"

"We're going to summer school," Charlotte says.

"Okay? Not the mall. We've been to the mall *once* together. We're going to French class. *Parlez-vous français?*" she asks, and I notice that her accent is actually, amazingly, improving.

Kamikaze starts talking in French, and I don't understand a word he says. When he sees how confused we look, he says, "I drove a bus in Montreal for a while. Now sit down."

When we get to class, we find out Monsieur LeFleur now has car trouble.

"He's survived some sort of horribly disabling flu, he's lost a member of his family, and now he's going to let a busted starter keep him from teaching our class?" someone asks.

"He could call a cab. He could take the bus—like us," Charlotte says.

We all sit there at our desks, feeling small and pathetic.

He hates us. It's obvious. He's not even in town this summer. He's sitting on a beach in southern France, sipping wine and laughing as he thinks about us, the fools in his Edison High summer-school class.

"Today, Monsieur LeFleur thought you could absorb a little French culture and some of the language by watching an Academy Award–winning movie," the sub says. "It's called *The French Connection*. Has anyone seen it?"

Nobody has.

"Then you're . . ." The sub skims the note she received from Monsieur LeFleur, then glances at the back of the video box. "You're in for some nonstop action, featuring the best car-chase scene in movie history."

"Is it a French car?" Charlotte asks.

"Well, no. I don't think so," the sub says.

"Then what's the point? I mean, what's the connection to French?" Charlotte demands.

"This is *supposed* to be French class," I say angrily. "Why aren't we watching a French movie, at least? Doesn't anyone care that we're not learning anything?"

"Girls, relax. This movie features some French characters. It has subtitles and everything," the sub says. She taps me and then Charlotte lightly on the head as she walks past, as if we're small children, as if patting us on the head will solve anything. Duck, duck, cut it out.

The movie is rated R—the kind of movie they don't allow us to see in school. Parents would definitely protest this. Some students protest by actually getting up and walking out of class.

Charlotte falls asleep during the exciting chase scene, where Gene Hackman is driving underneath the elevated subway tracks, racing the train. I close my eyes and picture myself racing through the streets of New York. I drive as well as Gene Hackman and then I apprehend the evil French killer when he gets off the train. Only I catch him

206

in French. I don't know how you shoot bullets *en français*, but that's what I do.

Then I stay in New York and get a very cool apartment.

When I open my eyes, I see that both the sub and Charlotte have dozed off in the afternoon heat.

Fireworks

It's the Fourth of July and it's almost dark. I am supposed to be meeting Charlotte right now, to go to the fireworks together.

Instead I'm at the town park's playground with Dorothy, Torvill, and Dean. Mom is doing a remote, a live broadcast from the big event, so she's perched at a table in the middle of the war memorial plaza. People keep stopping by to request songs and pick up free bumper stickers, and they all keep asking when she's due. I got tired of watching strangers touch her belly and listening to them predict whether she's having a girl or a boy.

Dad isn't here because he got some special session at the rink, because no one in their right mind wants to practice on a national holiday except Ludmila and Dad. He's supposedly going to meet me at the KLDV booth at 8:30, and then I get to find Charlotte in the huge crowd.

My parents make my life so complicated. They really do.

I told them I already had plans. But no. I'm pushing Torvill on a swing. I'm watching Dean climb on the jungle gym. I'm helping Dorothy create a sand sculpture. I'm trying really hard not to take how annoyed I am with my parents out on the kids, because it's not their fault our parents don't have a clue about how *not* to act on the Fourth of July.

"Just tell KLDV you can't do it!" I said to Mom when she came home this afternoon and informed me she had to work tonight.

"Just tell Ludmila you don't care if she doesn't celebrate July Fourth—you do!" I said to Dad.

"Peggy, honestly, we're only talking about one night here," my mother said. "Does one night really matter that much?"

In a word? Yes. Especially when it follows an afternoon, and a morning. But try telling my parents that. "I already promised Charlotte I'd go to the fireworks with her," I said. "I'm supposed to meet her at work."

"So call her and tell her to meet you at the park," my father said. "I'll be there by eight-thirty, I *promise*."

Yes, and that really means a lot these days.

"Dorothy shouldn't be out that late, should she?" I asked. "Shouldn't she be home?"

"It's just one night," my mother said. "Anyway, do you think she could actually sleep when fireworks are going off?"

They have an answer for everything. It's another gift of theirs.

At 8:25 I get the kids assembled and we circle back to the KLDV booth, but Dad's not there yet. So I take the kids with me to the place where I'm meeting Charlotte—at the top of the hill, near the statues of Lindville's founding fathers. As I crest the hill, I don't see Charlotte. I don't believe what I do see. It's Steve, leaning against one of the statues. And for the first time all summer, he is actually alone. Jacqui is nowhere to be seen.

So here it is, my moment. Me and Steve, alone. Except I'm not alone. Torvill and Dean are toddling along beside me, and I've got Dorothy on my shoulders.

I wave hello to Steve and walk over to him. I'm about to say something when the fireworks start going off. The first one makes a loud hissing noise, pops, and then nothing happens. No lights come out of it. It falls with a pathetic sigh, a complete dud.

Steve and I look at each other and start laughing. "Typical, right?" I ask him.

"Oh, yeah," he agrees. "So this is how Lindville celebrates July Fourth. Why am I not surprised?"

I laugh again, probably a little too hard, but I'm sorry—it's funny. There's a delay in the fireworks display, so they must be working on fixing something. "So have you seen Charlotte around here?" I ask Steve. "I'm supposed to be meeting her."

"Nope. Not yet," he says.

"Oh. Well, where's Jacqui?" I ask. I keep an eye on the twins as they chase each other, doing figure eights around the two statues.

"She had to work. Did Kyle have to work, too?" he says.

"Um, I guess so, yeah," I say. I haven't actually talked to Mike. And right now, I don't want to. "Hey, you know what? We actually got to watch a movie in French class the other day. Have you seen *The French Connec*—"

My sentence is interrupted as more fireworks are launched into the air. They explode with what seems like double force, as if they're trying to make up for the dud. There's a giant boom that nearly shakes the earth.

Torvill starts shrieking and crying, and runs away, heading straight for Mom and the KLDV booth. Dean chases after her, and then I have to leave Steve and bolt after both of them, which isn't easy with Dorothy on my shoulders. "I'll be right back!" I call to Steve. "Don't go anywhere, okay?"

He just waves as I hurry away. In the sky, bright red-white-and-blue stars flutter down. Dorothy holds out her hands and tries to catch them.

By the time we get to the booth and find Mom, Dad is there, too. "What happened?" he asks as he picks up Torvill and hugs her and tries to calm her down.

"That really loud one scared her," I say.

"Where were you? Why didn't you just wait here with your mother?"

"Um . . . because I have a life?" I say. Or at least, I'm trying to.

"What?" he asks.

"Nothing." I crouch down so that Dorothy can climb off of my shoulders. "Anyway, I'm late—I'm going to meet Charlotte. See you at home!" I rush off up the hill, eager to get back to Steve. We can still have our moment. This time, there won't be kids, there won't be Jacqui or Mike, there won't be . . .

Steve's not at the statue anymore.

"Sorry. Couldn't stall him long enough," Charlotte says, coming up to me. "He told me you were here but you had to run off after the kids. Sorry I'm late; it took me forever to get here."

"Traffic?"

"No. Slow vehicle," she says.

"Wait a second. I thought it was the car-of-the-month club night."

"Yeah. Well, Mom changed her mind. She said there are too many accidents on holidays."

"So, how did you get here?" I ask her.

"How do you think? The golf cart." She grins. "I mean, *le cart de golf*," she says.

I laugh. "I think you mean *la* cart," I correct her.

"Wait—that's it. We'll travel *à la cart*."

"Oh, wow. That's so perfect." Charlotte and I both step back and look up at the fireworks lighting up the sky.

With each explosion of fireworks I scan the crowd, looking for Steve. Where did he go? How could he vanish so quickly? And why do I care, when he so clearly does not? I see faces bathed in red, white, and blue. But not his.

"Look—there's Mike," Charlotte says. She points across the lawn. Two figures are heading our way.

"And Ray's with him," I observe.

"I don't want to see Ray," Charlotte says. "I'm not really sure if that's how I want to spend my evening. You know?"

"Well, I don't want to see Mike," I say. "It's going to be weird. You know? And I just . . ." I get this really nervous, sick feeling in my stomach, like I shouldn't have kissed him the other night, because I'm still too hung up on Steve, but if I see him again I'll probably do the same thing.

Charlotte and I look at each other for a second.

"It *is* Independence Day," I say.

"My mom is picking me up at Shady Prairies later— she could give you a ride home. Do you need to go tell your parents you're leaving?"

"No, I said I'd meet them at home," I tell her.

"Then let's go!" she says. I follow Charlotte, and we race toward where she's parked the cart a few blocks away.

We laugh as we dodge people, coolers, picnic baskets, dogs, kids. We leap into the golf cart, and Charlotte jams it into forward gear. We come out from underneath a clump of bushes like we're superheroes on a mission, except that we have bristly needles stuck in our hair and our vehicle only goes ten miles per hour.

As we go down an alley, trying to beat traffic and stay unseen, we nearly run into a man who is taking out the trash. He shakes his fist at us as we buzz on down the alley, doing our impression of an exciting getaway.

When we pull into Shady Prairies, Charlotte starts driving around the retirement-home property, giving me the grand tour.

"Shouldn't we just park?" I ask.

She doesn't respond. She heads up a sidewalk to the pool in the center courtyard, between all of the buildings. We hear a car honk a few times, and look at each other, panicked. "Security!" Charlotte whispers. She jerks the wheel to the right to turn around.

But she makes the turn too fast, and the pool deck is slick with evening dew. The cart suddenly tilts awkwardly to the right. "No!" Charlotte gasps as the cart tips all the way over onto its side, and we land sideways in lukewarm, chlorinated water.

I push myself out of the cart and swim to the surface. Actually I don't have to swim—I can just stand up. We careened into the very shallow end, and it's lucky we didn't hit our heads when we landed in the pool.

I grab my backpack from the submerged cart. Charlotte is already wading to the steps to climb out. She looks over at me and I don't know whether to laugh or cry. How did this happen? How did we end up here? We are so dead.

"We've got to get this thing out of here," she says, and we try to drag the cart out of the pool, but it's impossible.

"No, *we've* got to get out of here," I say, "before anyone sees us."

We run from the pool, shaking ourselves like wet dogs, trying to dry a little before her mother comes to get us. The night is so hot that it shouldn't take long.

"All right, Fleming," Charlotte says as we sit on an unlighted bench out front. "Start thinking of a story for when someone asks. Because they're going to ask."

I nod, wringing out the bottom of my T-shirt. "A story. Sure."

She's Uncomfortable

"I've only got a few minutes to do this," my father says when we sit down at his desk on Friday morning. He's home briefly, between final practice and a house closing, and my mother's upstairs, because she just started her maternity leave. My father jiggles the pencil cup on his desk. "So. Let's see what you've got."

I hand him a check. I'm glad he doesn't have much time. After what happened last night, I don't want to be around my parents too much. I might feel guilty, crack under the pressure, and tell them everything.

"Another hundred. Very good, P. F." He makes a note on the sheet of paper titled P. F.: Personal Loan, then looks up at me. "But I thought you were giving me one-fifty this week."

"I was. I meant to," I say.

"Okay. Tell me what happened." He looks me straight in the eye.

I panic for a few seconds. Is he talking about *everything*? "Well, I sort of forgot to budget—"

"P. F. The truth," he says.

I open my mouth, not even sure what I'm about to confess, when the phone on his desk rings, saving me. He answers it and then hands it to me.

"Fleming! Oh, my God. I have to talk to you," Charlotte says breathlessly.

"Oh . . . hey, Charlotte," I say. I glance across the desk at Dad. "Charlotte," I mouth to him. "Just be a minute."

He looks at his watch and then taps it to remind me he's in a hurry.

"Is this a good time?" Charlotte asks. "Can you talk?"

"No."

"Oh. Your dad's right there, huh? Well, someone from work just called with this incredible story—I've got to tell you."

"Mm-hmm," I say, afraid of what she'll say next.

"So at six-o'clock breakfast they opened the blinds in the dining room, and there was this really bright metal thing glinting in the sun, beaming right back into the dining room, hurting everyone's eyes. It was the cart. The sun was reflecting off it in the pool. So far everyone thinks it was some resident who wandered out of the Alzheimer's nursing-home division—we're cool. Talk to you later!" She hangs up, leaving me with a racing pulse and a lot of questions.

"Okay, bye, see you at class—and thanks!" I place the phone back into its holder.

"P. F. It's Friday," my father says. "You don't have class today."

"Oh." I slump a little in my chair, hoping this isn't the beginning of my unraveling.

"So, let's see, we subtract a hundred, and your remaining debt comes to four hundred. Wow, P. F. You're doing very—"

Suddenly my mother lets out a loud, hysterical shriek, and then shouts, "Come quick! Come quick!"

We both jump up and run for the stairs. The kids abandon their Lego sculpture in the living room and follow us. "Oh, no," my father says. "This is *not* the day to have the baby."

"What are you talking about?" I say. "*I'm* the one who has to—has to—" When I start thinking this is the actual delivery we're talking about, I can't talk. I can't breathe normally. I'm almost hyperventilating.

Mom is propped up on their bed watching TV. Her feet are on a pillow, and she's sipping water from a bottle cradled in her arms.

"Look!" she says as we skid into the bedroom. "Isn't that where Charlotte works?"

A reporter is wrapping up a story from Shady Prairies. This is big because Lindville is never on TV, unless there's severe weather. It takes a tornado, or at least a gale-force wind, for them to send out a satellite truck.

There are dozens of senior citizens crowded around the pool. The reporter is saying that there has been a head count and that one person is missing from the complex. They seem to think the missing person and the flipped cart are connected.

"Gee, I hope nobody got hurt," Mom says as the kids climb onto the bed with her. "What if someone hit their head?"

"Did Charlotte tell you about that just now?" my father asks.

"No." I shake my head. "She hasn't gone to work yet—she works nights," I say. That, and the fact that she didn't have to tell me about it, because I was there.

"Hmm. Well, I've got to run, or I'm going to be late," my father says.

"Peggy, you're going to help me clean the house today, right? While the kids nap?" my mother asks after my father kisses her good-bye and rushes down the stairs.

"I am?" I say. I thought maternity leave meant I was now off the hook—not more on it.

"Yes. I was hoping we could do some relaxation exercises, too. This heat is really making me uncomfortable," she says as she shifts position on the bed. "So what on earth do you think happened at Shady Prairies?"

Her. *She's* uncomfortable.

Love among the Pancakes

I'm restocking the napkin dispenser Saturday night at work when Ray's truck pulls up outside at the pump. I stare out the window at the truck, wondering what Ray is up to tonight. I really hope he isn't going to come in and punch Denny for giving Charlotte some tapes. Denny's nose is already crooked, and we both know he's not the best fighter in town.

Ray gets out to pump the gas. The passenger-side door opens and Mike gets out. He peers at the gas station, and there I am, staring right out at him. He waves and then jogs toward me, looking happy to see me.

"So, Fleming. Where've you *been*?" Mike asks when he walks into the store. He's wearing his usual red flip-flops.

"Around," I say, feeling nervous.

"Around, huh? What have you been doing?" He comes up really close to me and when I look in his eyes, I start remembering the car wash.

Behind me, I hear Denny humming. I wish he'd turn up the radio so that he can't eavesdrop.

"Well, I've been busy. Really busy," I say as I fidget with my stupid apron. "My family . . . and the job . . . and the new baby coming . . . and . . . " I shrug. "You know."

"Yeah. I've been busy, too. You wouldn't believe how many people order pizza during a heat wave," Mike says. "It was *insane* on the Fourth. So do you have a break or something coming up?"

"Um . . ." I'm about to say no when for some reason I look right at Mike's mouth, and I remember how kissing him was sort of thrilling, the feel-good movie of the summer so far. Without another thought, I hang up my apron, ask Denny to cover for me for a couple of minutes, and Mike and I head out back. Denny glares at me the entire time it takes to walk past him. It's like having an extra father around.

"Is this okay with Ray?" I ask as we go out the back door.

"Sure. He's cool," Mike says.

I prop the door open with an empty container of 10W-30 motor oil, then turn to find Mike. In the dark, I stumble over some discarded cardboard boxes on the ground and Mike catches my arm. He puts his arm around my waist and pulls me close, right up against him.

"Careful," he says. "You're as bad as me trying to Rollerblade."

221

"That bad? Really?" I tease him.

"Hey, not all of us are born skaters, okay?" Mike smiles, and in the deserted area behind the store, I notice how white his teeth are. I haven't been back here except to toss trash bags into the Dumpster. It smells horrible. I try to close off my nose, to stop breathing, to stop absorbing the noxiousness.

"A born skater? Interesting," I say, glancing down at my feet.

His hands are on my hips and he pulls me toward him again and kisses me. His lips don't feel the same as they did that night in the car wash—they're dry, maybe a little sunburned or windburned. Then again, it's hard to kiss while I'm also holding my breath to avoid Dumpster smells.

"You know what's bizarre?" Mike pauses to look at me. He runs his fingers up and down my bare arms. "Gropher is, like, the biggest liar in the world. I mean, usually nothing he says is true."

"Oh, yeah?" I say. "Really?" I hadn't thought of him as a liar before.

"Are you serious? The dude has made up almost everything," Mike says.

"Like what?" I challenge him.

"Like all that stuff about gambling and being an addict and all. He's never lost big at gambling. He's played poker like *twice* in his life, and he sucked at it," Mike says.

222

"I beat him. My father beat him."

"Really?" I ask. I can't believe it. Everyone at school thinks he's on his tenth step.

"That scar he says he got from jumping off a roof? Okay, he fell off his bike or something. Going down a hill and turning too fast. I mean, he's just . . . he takes stuff and he makes it sound like something else."

"Really?" I say again.

"He's supposed to be saving all that money from waiting tables for his road trip? Then explain how he owns like a thousand CDs and DVDs. You know what I mean?"

My heart starts to sink a little—no, a lot. Or maybe it just didn't have that far down to go.

Steve was supposed to take French, but he didn't. Maybe all his talk about getting out of Lindville is just that: talk. Because if you look at it one way, it does seem as if maybe he's working really hard toward being the IHOP manager here, instead of toward escaping town.

Mike moves closer to me and kisses my neck. "Anyway, that's beside the point. Because even though he lies? The really cool thing is, everything he said about you is true."

"About me?" I step back from Mike. "What about me is true?" I ask him, and at the same time I don't want to know.

Mike kisses my neck again. "He said you were a really

223

good kisser. He said even though you weren't his type, he just felt like he had to kiss you again, after the first time."

I stare at him, this awful burning in my throat. "Oh, yeah? I'm not his *type*? When did he say that?"

"I don't know. Who cares? The point is, he was right," Mike says. He tries to kiss me again, and I shove him away, nearly knocking him against the Dumpster.

"What? It's a compliment," Mike says.

I go back inside, tossing the plastic oil container aside, and I close the door behind me, which locks it. Then I realize that anyone, even Mike, can walk into the front of the store as long as it's open, so it doesn't matter whether I close that door or not.

"I don't want to talk about it," I say before Denny can ask. Headlights flash against the windows and I glance out and see Mike and Ray driving away.

I take some bleach and cleanser and start scrubbing the sink, one of the chores Jamie left for me. I can't stop thinking about how I was so stupid, how this whole thing got so ridiculous. I kept thinking that Steve and I had this connection, because of the way we met and the things we talked about. I thought we were . . . soul mates or something. I figured he was only with Jacqui because they worked together and that kind of stuff happens when you work with someone. Or so I've heard. It isn't happening here at Gas 'n Git, which is fine by me.

Anyway, it turns out Steve never meant anything he

said, that he's so shallow he believes in "types," and that he liked kissing me—enough to tell Mike about it—and that's it. He made out with me and then reported on it. Which I would have thought was really beneath him. But now I guess it's obvious that I don't know him at all.

Now I know two things I didn't want to: that Steve isn't interested in me, even though he likes making out with me, and that Mike probably only came after me because of what Steve said about my kissing . . . skill, or whatever you'd call it. I guess I can't be mad at Mike, though I am. I only went out with him because I wanted to get to Steve.

We're thwarted all around.

Denny walks over and puts a fruit drink on my counter. "With my compliments," he says. "That is, if you can drink anything after inhaling all those bleach fumes."

I laugh, and for a second forget how angry and upset and furious I feel.

"So the guy's a loser. You realize that."

"He's not the problem," I say. "There's this other guy—his best friend, Steve. I sort of used to . . . I don't know." I can't say I ever dated him, can I? "Anyway, he's going out with this other girl now. They both work at IHOP."

"Love among the pancakes," Denny says dryly. "How romantic."

"I have to leave work a little early tonight," I say. I flip open the phone book and look up *Taxi*.

"Okay, I'll tell people we're out of coffee. But be careful." Denny looks at me and I can tell he knows what I'm about to do. "Don't slip on any butter pats."

Back When I Was Delusional

Lindville Limousine drops me at IHOP precisely at 11:00 P.M. I'm not in a limousine, I'm in a green van, but the driver assures me that she can make my arrival look fancy if I want, not seeming to notice that I'm wearing a T-shirt and jeans, which is not even a good outfit for what I have planned. The driver keeps a red carpet in the back, she tells me, for just such occasions.

"Don't worry, this isn't prom night," I tell her. "Not even close."

"All righty. How long are you going to be?"

"I'm not sure," I say. "Five minutes?"

"Tell you what. I could use some coffee, so how about I turn off the meter and we meet back here in five?" she says.

"That would be great," I tell her. I get out of the cab and face the restaurant building. The parking lot is almost full.

I remember Steve telling me that he worked on Saturday nights because the restaurant is busy and he makes a lot in tips. That's one of the reasons I agreed to work at Gas 'n Git Saturday nights, back when I was living in fantasyland, back when I thought we'd go out this summer, back when I was delusional.

I walk into the restaurant with my head held high. The hostess station is vacant, so I decide to seat myself. I spot Steve heading for the kitchen, and I'm about to walk over to him when Jacqui rushes up in front of me.

"Oh, hi, Fleming. It's you," she says. "What are you doing here so late?"

"You're going to seat me in Steve's section," I say.

She stares at me. "What?"

"Just do it. Don't ask questions," I say. I pick up a menu from the stack on the hostess station and shove it into her hands. "Let's go."

Jacqui glances over her shoulder at me three times as she takes me to a booth, as if I'm dangerously unbalanced and need to be watched. She places the menu on the table and steps away slowly, guardedly. "Steve will be your server tonight," she says robotically. Then she turns and nearly sprints back to the hostess station, to help my cabdriver.

I don't open the menu, because I know it by heart and because I'm not planning on ordering.

I'm also not planning on sitting here in the future, wishing something would happen with Steve.

I look around as I wait for him to come out of the

kitchen. Maybe Jacqui has told him that I'm sitting in his section and I'm acting crazy. Maybe he's already talked to Mike. Maybe he won't *ever* come out.

As I rehearse what I've planned to say, which is woeful and dramatic and unrealistic, I look around at the other tables. The customers seated at them are here for fun occasions, or at least occasions, or at the very least, pancakes. They're not here for the same reason I am. That much is for sure.

Suddenly there's a blue apron in my field of vision. "Hello, my name is Steve and . . ."

"And you're a complete and utter jerk," I say. I look up at Steve. He's dyed his blond hair sort of pink since the last time I saw him. What is up with that? Is he taking hair-dye lessons from the bleached-blond plastic girl?

"What?" he says.

The rest of my witty and devastating speech vanishes as I look at him. I stare at the menu for a second to reorient myself. "I talked to Mike tonight," I tell him.

"Oh, yeah? Well, cool," Steve says, looking flustered. "I mean, you guys are sort of like together now, so—"

"No, we're not!" I say, a little too loudly for the general IHOP diner. "We're not *together*."

"Um . . ." Steve bounces up and down on his toes a little. "Fleming? What's this all about? What's the deal?" I don't say anything, and he sits on the edge of the booth bench across from me and looks at me nervously.

"I guess . . ." I look down and realize that I'm tearing my napkin into shreds. "Look. I thought you were different. And I thought we . . . I thought you . . ." I stop for a minute. This isn't what I rehearsed. But I'm not going to blow it.

"I know we just made out a couple of times, but I always really liked you," I say. "I thought you liked me, too. A little, anyway. I thought we had this connection. I thought we were going places together, not as in go places, you know, achieve great things, but literally go, get out of town, see other states, cities." The Christie Farrell talking gene strikes at the most inopportune moments. "But now I find out you lied about everything, you never planned on taking French, you aren't buying a truck, or a van, you aren't going anywhere. You just liked making out with me. That's it? And you tell your friends they should go after me because I can kiss good? Kiss *well*, I mean. No, wait—not just good. Really, really *good* well?"

"What?" Steve just sits there, looking stunned.

"Well, don't I?" I ask.

I'm an idiot to ask this. I know that, but it still comes out.

"Sure. Yes," Steve says. He glances around the general area, and a man waves a coffee pitcher in the air, asking for more. "Um, I sort of have to—"

"You're such a hypocrite!" I cut him off, not done yet. "We totally hit it off, and you liked kissing me—but you can't go out with me because I'm not your *type*? Instead you want to go out with *her*?" I practically scream as I throw my arm out to point at Jacqui. "She's your type?"

A busboy is walking by with a tray full of dishes and he veers away at the last second, avoiding a crash.

That's when I realize that I don't know whether I'm sitting here begging and humiliating myself, or whether I'm finally standing up for myself and telling him what *I* want. And what's the difference, really?

"So did you want to order anything?" Steve asks. "I mean, maybe we could talk on my break. I'm not sure, because we're sort of busy tonight, but—"

"No. I can't stay. I don't want to talk. I just—I thought you were different," I say as I get to my feet. "I don't know why. But you're not. And I don't even know what I'm doing here." I start to run for the door.

"Hey! Are you skipping out on the check?" Jacqui yells after me.

Dine and dash, Charlotte told me once. But this isn't what she meant. I leap into the waiting cab and tell the driver my home address.

"Denny said you left work in a cab. Where have you been?" My mother and father are sitting outside on the front steps, with the door ajar so they can listen to the kids inside.

"What are you doing out here?" I ask, grateful that

Denny didn't tell my father where I went. I can just imagine my dad running into IHOP in his skating gear, shaking his fist at me.

The Lindville Limousine driver pulls away with a friendly good-night wave. From the looks on my parents' faces, maybe I should whistle for the taxi to come back.

"I can't sleep. My back hurts and I'm too huge," my mother says. "And your father just got home from driving around, looking for you after you weren't at Gas 'n Git and you didn't show up here."

"So where were you?" my father asks.

"I can't explain right now," I say.

"Yes, you can, and you're going to," my father says. "P. F., what's going on? You're worrying us."

"It's nothing," I say.

"Nothing? Then how about answering our questions? You're spending money to take a cab. Why? Where did you go?"

"Look, I had a really bad night," I say. "I'm only half an hour late, and I don't want to talk about it."

My father stands up. "Maybe not, but you're going to."

I can't tell them that I had to go confront someone I've been obsessing over. "I had to take a cab," I say, "because you won't let me drive. Sometimes there are places I have to go that I don't want you to take me to. And I can't skate there, at night, and there's no buses at night, and I can't get a ride. So that's why. It's the first time I've done it, and it cost me twenty-one dollars, and I don't plan on doing it again, okay?"

My father's staring at me and blinking rapidly. I can tell that he's reached his personal boiling point—I've seen him like this before. "Fine," he says. "But we still want to know where you went in that cab. If you don't tell us, we'll call the cab company. It's not that hard."

"Fine. Go ahead," I say. "Call them. Whatever. I'm tired." I walk into the house and go upstairs to get ready for bed. While I'm brushing my teeth, I hear my mother and father in the hallway, talking. I can't hear what they're saying, but I know it's about me.

The Skating of the Lambs

My father's first performance is at 7:00 on the opening night of Rodeo Roundup Days. It costs four tickets to see him, which means Dad is worth more than the petting zoo but less than the Ferris wheel.

I look nervously around the bleachers as we sit down, to see if anyone I know is here. So far I recognize some kids from school, and several of my parents' friends. Mr. Stinson is rinkside, with a few other Lindville bigwigs.

I look around the non–regulation-size rink, which they didn't exactly finish closing off the way they were supposed to. There's a new roof to keep out the sun, and both ends and one side of the building are completed; but one side is only half done, covered with a chain-link fence and chicken wire, with random boards nailed to it. This goes with the decorating theme, because they've also nailed wooden boards against the rink's interior to make it look like a corral. Generators are whirring loudly, trying to keep the ice and the rink area cold.

There's a concession stand just outside the rink and a hawker yelling, "Get your frozen lemonade right here!" Torvill and Dean keep bugging me, then Mom, then me again, for frozen lemonade. Dorothy is sitting beside me patiently, waiting for the program to begin.

Dad told us not to come tonight; in fact he almost sounded like he was begging us not to. I seriously considered skipping this. For one thing, I don't want to run into either Mike or Steve at the rodeo. For another, I don't think Lindville's going to appreciate my dad's skating, and I feel a major embarrassment coming on. And for still another, it's very awkward to be here with my mother, to watch my father, when they're both still mad at me from Saturday night.

But I can't not be here. You don't want to miss any of Dad's performances. There's always something really incredible about each one of them—he'll throw in a difficult jump at the last second, when he's got the crowd on his side and things are clicking along. He'll draw them in, have them clapping to the music, and then afterward the ice will be littered with roses and stuffed animals. At least that's what used to happen, in all the videotapes I've seen of him competing. I don't know about tonight. The ice might be littered with something else, I think as I look at the three lambs and two horses standing on the ice, posed as part of the cowboy scene. Fortunately Dad doesn't have to skate with the animals—just around them.

My father is wearing a red-checked gingham shirt and pants that look like brown suede, only they're fake and made out of stretchy material that won't split when he jumps. The pants actually have real suede fringe running down the side seams. He's wearing a black ten-gallon hat, and black skates that match it. Mr. Stinson must be so proud, I think.

The temperature outside is still in the eighties. To help the ice stay frozen, they've dumped in tons and tons of cubed ice and tried to smooth it over, so my father has to skate on a melting and bumpy surface. It's impossible to skate well on soft ice. The performance is going to be a disaster—in more ways than one.

Dad has to round up the lambs as he skates around them and leaps over bales of hay, while two rodeo clowns with shoes on slide on the ice and fall down. The rodeo clowns look like some of the people Dad used to skate with in the ice shows. So much makeup, so little time. This is a step down, not just for my dad, but for the rodeo clowns, too. They're professionals. They keep bulls from killing riders. They don't goof around on skating rinks. I hope they're getting paid overtime for this.

I don't know what the horses are for, but at least they'll go with the country music the rodeo guys insisted Dad use, after they said first our alternative-rock medley and then Denny's U2 mix was too rebellious for Rodeo

Roundup Days. They ended up handing Dad a tape and saying he had to use the three songs on it. "So much for artistic interpretation," Dad said when he showed me the tape.

At exactly 7:00 there's an announcement from the audio booth. "Ladies and gentlemen, introducing the one . . . the only . . . Phil Farrell in 'Cowboy Bo Peep'!"

Torvill and Dean shriek with excitement and the audience applauds as the music begins: first, just a harmonica playing a sad cowboy ballad, as my father steps onto the ice and circles around. He stops to joke with the rodeo clowns and circles the rink while a horrible voice-over from a grizzled old cowhand goes on about "the life of a lonely cowboy."

Then the real music starts: It's a medley that kicks off with a high-energy Garth Brooks song called—appropriately—"Rodeo." The crowd loves it and Dad plays to them, smiling and clapping as he does tricky footwork and makes his way up and down the ice. Then he grabs a lasso from one of the rodeo clowns and tries to make rope circles as he skates, only he can't do it, and the clown chases him and shows him how to do it right. People laugh, but then settle into watching Dad as he tosses the lasso away and builds speed, skates forward, does a quick double Axel. He moves so quickly and gracefully, especially considering he has to skate around livestock. Dad jumps over a bale of hay and the crowd gasps, then applauds. He does a double toe loop and then a triple flip, and even the sheep look impressed.

Suddenly, outside the rink, there's a huge commotion. People are screaming, and there's the sound of thundering hooves. Everyone in the bleacher seats turns around to look out the open side of the rink. I see a giant black bull go rushing past, on the loose—completely out of control.

"Insane Zane's escaped!" a woman screams.

"He's gone crazy from the heat!" a man behind us yells.

The rodeo clowns bolt off the ice and sprint after Insane Zane. Cowboys ride past the rink, in hot pursuit, throwing ropes to try to lasso him. He's one of the meanest, toughest bulls, and it's a big challenge every year to see who can stay on him the longest. Apparently no one could stay on him—or with him—tonight.

When the noise subsides and we all turn back around, my father has stopped skating. He stares dejectedly at the horses and the sheep. He looks completely baffled, like he doesn't know how he ended up doing this or how to make sense of it. My heart really goes out to him—this isn't how his first performance should go, no matter how inane it is.

"He hates having his program interrupted," Mom says as Dad steps off the ice.

"I know," I say.

Mom turns to me. "I wasn't saying that for your benefit. I was explaining to the little ones."

"The little ones don't understand, so what's the point?" I say.

"Peggy, what is *with* you? Your attitude is terrible," Mom says.

How could it not be? I'm stuck at the rodeo with my family.

The crowd gasps and shouts as Insane Zane rushes past the rink again. Dean suddenly jumps out of his seat and scampers down the rows of bleachers.

"Dean, come back!" Mom yells. "Come back here right now!"

But Dean either doesn't hear her or doesn't care. He lands on the bottom bleacher and races for the exit.

I go after Dean before Mom can tell me to go after him. That would just really irritate me right now. I catch up with him just outside the door. Insane Zane is racing around the concession stand and knocks down both the frozen lemonade cart and the Boots for Sale booth. Dean darts toward the bull before I can grab his shirt. I run after Dean, even though people are shouting at us to get back. Above our heads, ropes are flying as the cowboys attempt to lasso the bull's horns.

Insane Zane stops racing and slowly trots toward us. He has a black coat, and seems about as long as a railroad car. He's taller than I am, wider than I am, and has long, sharp-looking horns and stuff dripping out of his quarter-size nostrils. With those he should definitely be able to smell our fear, and anything else about us.

I decide not to look at him—staring at him might be challenging him in some way. I decide not to breathe. Then maybe he'll think I'm already dead. I step in front of Dean to shield him, but he jumps out and does a high karate kick, yelling "Hi-ya!"

At the same exact moment, three separate ropes circle Insane Zane's head, stopping him in his tracks. He stands there, staring at us, looking bewildered but still mad.

"Cool!" Dean says as the cowboys tighten the ropes and rein in the bull. "I got him. Did you see how I got him?"

I just drop to my knees and hug Dean for all he's worth. I'm shaking all over, and I squeeze Dean's tiny shoulders until I stop.

"I'm going to be a cowboy," Dean says. "Peggy, let me go; I'm a cowboy." I release him and he runs around kicking the air and pretending to lasso things with an imaginary rope.

"Sure you are," I say. "Of course you are."

When we go back inside the rink, Mom wants to know what took us so long. Dad is smiling and playing to the crowd as he skates down the ice, doing some fancy footwork, snapping his fingers to the country beat.

What Boy?

We wait for Dad by the burgers, ribs, and pork-chop-on-a-stick stands for a quick snack after his eight-o'clock show. I desperately hope his second show went better than his first.

I've gone on two rides with Torvill and Dean, because Mom can't. She's letting the kids stay out late tonight, but she's the one who looks completely beat. Mom is sleepily eating a half slab of ribs, Torvill has corn on the cob, and Dean a grape Popsicle. Dorothy has fallen asleep in her stroller, which isn't like her at all. I stand at the end of the picnic table and keep looking around for Charlotte and Denny, who are supposed to meet me either here or over by the Scrambler ride.

"Peggy, have a seat—there's room," Mom says, patting the bench beside her.

"That's okay," I say. "I'm actually not going to be here much longer."

"What do you mean?"

"I'm meeting my friends. We're going to hang out here for a while," I say.

"But that's impossible. You can't go hang out late with your friends tonight."

"Why not?" I ask. "Mom, the rodeo's only here for ten days. It's the only time anything ever happens here. So can't you let me enjoy it?"

"That's not it. You never *mentioned* you were meeting Charlotte," Mom says.

"Well, I'm mentioning it now."

"What boy is it this time?" Mom asks. I start to shake my head, but she insists. "No, really, what boy?"

"There's no boy," I say.

"Do you expect me to believe that? After Saturday night?" Mom says.

Just then, Dad comes over to join us, carrying a dish of fried pickles and wearing clogs with his cowboy costume. As he gets closer, I see he's got makeup on, too.

Dean runs up and tells him how he took down the runaway bull, how he stopped Insane Zane. "That's nice," Dad says, distracted. "The second program went much better. This thing with the animals . . . it's a learning curve, I guess," he says as he crunches into a deep-fried pickle spear.

"Well, Peggy is now going out with her friends," Mom says in an angry tone, before I can tell him how well he skated, how he made something decent out of nothing.

"Yes, I am," I say, staring at her.

"Hey, Fleming." I turn around and Denny is standing behind me. He has this knack for coming to my rescue.

"Hey," I say, turning toward him. "Have you seen Charlotte?"

"Not yet, but I'm kind of early," Denny says. "Were we meeting by the food, or by the rides?"

"Here or at the Scrambler," I say. "Should we go over there now?"

Mom sets down her ribs and wipes her face and that's when I know she's getting serious. "You're not going anywhere with him."

"Mom, he's a friend," I say.

"I asked what boy and you said there's no boy," Mom says.

"My *friend*. Denny. The guy I work with," I say. "You and Dad even met him at our house," I remind her.

"So. Does that mean I know anything about him?" she says.

She's picking a really bad time to all of a sudden get involved in my life again.

"Fleming, I'll meet you over there, then," Denny says. He takes off, and I know how he feels. No one wants to be around someone else's family fight.

"Why is he wearing sunglasses?" my father wonders. "It's almost dark. I don't trust him."

"That's not it—I don't trust *Peggy*," Mom says to him.

"It's Fleming, Mom," I say. "God, could you just try sometimes?"

"Could *I* try? Oh, that's good. That's really good." She rips open a second packet of hand wipes. "Fleming, then. I've been *trying* to keep you involved in this family. But it's like you don't even want to be involved."

My father sets his little container of fried pickles on the table. "Look, let's not make this bigger than it has to be. P. F., you can't hang out with your friends tonight and come home late again. You have class tomorrow. You work tomorrow. End of story."

"My French teacher has blown off every single class so far—we have subs who don't even speak French," I tell them. "Of course, you wouldn't know that because you don't ask how my class is going. And work? I'll be fine for work. I always am. Have I missed a day yet? Have I missed *anything* yet?"

"Yes. You've missed the last, like, five family nights in a row, so—"

"I have family night every day!" I say, which makes more sense than it sounds like. "I'm the one who's home while you guys are out skating and forecasting and remoting and whatever else you do when you strand me at home without a car."

"You know what? I know what this is all about," Mom says. She shakes her head and says quietly, "You can't stand the fact that you don't get all the attention now. That you've got a brother and sisters, and you're mad at us about that. You've never adjusted to this, so you're taking it out on us by running around with these guys this summer—"

"I'm not running around with anyone!" I say, which isn't completely true, but it's close. "Look, I have adjusted, I am adjusting, I am adjusted. Do you want me to conjugate this for you in French? If I had an actual teacher, maybe I could, but no, my summer sucks. My entire summer is about paying you back, and making good on my promises, which I'm doing. Can't you see that?"

"P. F., your entire summer hasn't been about paying us back," Dad says.

"No, actually, my entire summer has been about helping you guys out," I say. "Peggy, can you do this, Peggy, can you do that? Except you usually don't ask. You just assume. You totally take me for granted. You just make plans for me without me knowing about them."

"That's—that's not true," my father stammers. "We always ask."

"We're a family," my mother says. "Family means thinking about other people besides yourself, family means—"

"Family! Does family mean that you guys can completely forget about *me*, about what I might want? I've given up so much time to help you guys out, and you don't

245

even notice—you just cruise in when you want to, when KLDV doesn't need you, or some homeowner doesn't need you, or when the rink is closed because it's midnight. You expect me to take Lamaze class and figure out your skating program? And if you figure out your skating, and get your sponsors, you're going to *leave* for a few months on tour? Are you serious? Are you even thinking about anyone besides yourselves?"

"We *always* think about you," Mom says, looking stung, and Dad nods slowly in agreement, almost as if he doesn't know what I'm talking about.

"Right. You think about me when you're off deciding to have another child right before my senior year, and you think about me when you're off deciding to leave home and go on a skating tour during my senior year," I say angrily. "And you guys are always telling me how I have to learn to be more responsible—*me*."

All of a sudden I notice Dorothy has woken up and is staring up at me with these big, watery blue eyes, blinking, not understanding, not recognizing this tone of voice, about to burst into tears.

I can't take it. I can't see Dorothy cry right now. She never cries, and if she starts, then I might, too.

I quickly walk away, leaving the food booths. I go past all of the games of skill, looking through tear-blurred eyes at furry white bears and pandas hanging from strings, and metal ducks being shot to a hollow *ting ting ting* sound.

Steve is probably there, trying to win smelly stuffed animals for Jacqui, his *type*, but I don't want to know if he is. I don't want to see him—or anyone—right now. I can't believe my parents can just stand there and tell me how much they think of me, how considerate they are, how I'm the one who doesn't understand "family." They've got it all wrong. They're so different from how they used to be. The three of us used to be so close; we did everything together. Now it's the two of them—and I'm the nanny.

I pass the rodeo stadium. Inside, loudspeakers blare girls' barrel-racing results, and the crowd screams in excitement as the bareback bronco riding begins. Everyone's shouting and applauding and having a great time. Everyone except me.

When I get to the Scrambler, Charlotte and Denny are standing in line, waiting with tickets for me, too. I fake a smile and Charlotte says, "I heard you and your parents got into it. Everything okay?"

"No," I say.

"*Ew.* I mean, triple *ew.*" She hands me a wide silver-toned belt buckle with the initials PFF on it. She shrugs. "They were engraving them and I thought it looked cool."

"A warning," Denny says to me. "She's really into this rodeo thing."

"Thanks. Just don't make me pose for the caricature guy," I say. "Or those old-fashioned saloon-girl portraits."

"Come on!" Charlotte's jaw drops. "You are no fun."

247

"Oh, God. How did I let you guys talk me into this?" Denny says as he climbs into the Scrambler cart and closes the gate behind him, and the three of us are squashed together. "Do you know what this is going to do to my rep?"

"You *have* a rep?" I ask.

"Yes, she's alive! Fleming's alive!" Charlotte puts her arm around me and hugs tight.

She and Denny are laughing and talking about the parade tomorrow, but I don't really listen. The ride doesn't feel like it's been put together right, with metal scraping on metal as we revolve. I close my eyes so I don't have to look at the faces in the crowd watching us as we whip past, so I don't have to see if my parents came to find me or not.

Beaucoup Busted

Around 11:30 the next morning, Denny and I are watching the tiny black-and-white TV behind his register. We're taking a break because we've been mobbed with customers for the last five hours. When the Rodeo Roundup Days get into full swing, it's like this every day, all over town. Tourists wanting to buy everything. It keeps the town financially afloat for the rest of the year, but it's ten days of traffic jams and restocking soda. Jamie is even here to help, though she disappeared into her office about half an hour ago.

The lead story on the news is the rodeo parade that starts at noon. As I said, Lindville doesn't get onto TV often. We have to watch when it does.

"So," Denny says. "I haven't had time to ask yet. Did you and your parents talk when you got home last night?"

I've been so busy this morning that I've managed to sort of forget that my parents and I had a huge fight last night. I didn't see them after that. Denny dropped me off, a block from home, at about 10:30.

"Not really," I say. When I walked into the house last night, they were sitting in the living room, propped on opposite ends of the sofa, rubbing each other's feet. I looked at them, and then I went upstairs without saying anything. Later there was a knock on my door, but I didn't answer it. For all I know that could have been Dorothy, not my parents.

"No? Not at all?" Denny asks.

"No."

"Well, what was the fight *about*?"

"Nothing," I say.

Denny tosses his empty glass bottle into the recycling bin. "Fine. Be the most unloquacious coffee wench of the century, see if I care."

Jamie walks out from the office in the back. "What are you two doing? Just sitting here, watching TV?" She quickly checks all the coffee pumps. "We're running on empty here, and you're watching TV!"

"We were taking a break," Denny says.

Jamie starts to make coffee. "You get everything ready and *then* you take a break."

"Hey. I don't even work on that side, so don't yell at me," Denny says.

"I've got it," I say, rushing over to intervene before Jamie can ruin the brewing. I only have fifteen minutes left on my shift, and Kamikaze's coffee has to come out of this batch.

The phone rings and Denny answers it. "Gas 'n Git."

He holds the receiver away from his ear, and I hear a woman's hysterical voice. He slowly hands the phone to me. "Your mother. I think."

I grab the phone, wondering why Mom's calling here—she never does that. "Mom?"

"Peggy! I mean Fleming—*sorry*, Peg—I mean Fleming," Mom stammers. "I thought it was heat stroke, but then my water broke, and—it's time. My contractions are coming really close together and it doesn't make sense, the barometric pressure's over thirty, and I'm early, but . . . I'm on my way to the hospital . . . hurry and meet me there!"

"But Mom—can't you pick me up first?" I ask. "On the way?"

"No time! Baby coming fast . . . parade today . . . blocking streets off . . . now or never! Hurry, please!" She hangs up.

I feel panic grip me. I'm thinking in gasps; I'm not breathing right; It's time. For me. To help. Deliver a baby. My new brother. Or sister. I grab the counter to steady myself, to keep from keeling over.

"I—I have to go," I tell Denny as I fling off my sandals, grab my skates, and start jamming my toes into them. "She's having the baby. I have to be there."

"You're skating to the hospital?" Denny says. "No. Come on, Michelle Kwan. I'll drive you."

"What's going on?" Jamie asks.

"Fleming's mom is having a baby," Denny begins. "Fleming has to get to the hospital, so I'm going to drive her."

"No," Jamie says. "You can't."

"Why not?" Denny asks. "This is an emergency."

"The store can't be open with just one employee," Jamie says. "Gas 'n Git regulation. It's not safe! I'm sorry, I really am. But I can't have you both leave."

"But this is an emergency," Denny says again.

"Look, this might sound harsh, but Fleming isn't the one about to have a baby," Jamie says as she starts arranging the Muffins of the Month into a neat circle.

I pull at Denny's sleeve and tug him away from her. "Don't push it—it's fine, I can get there myself. Anyway, you're meeting Charlotte here in like ten minutes for the parade—remember?" They wouldn't stop discussing the plan last night.

Denny's just glaring at Jamie. "She's so obsessed with those stupid muffins. I feel like pegging her with one."

"Well, don't. We'll get fired."

"So?"

"So I don't want to get fired!" I say. "This is the only job I've had that I've kept, and I have to keep it so I can get out of debt, because if I don't get out of debt I'll owe my parents forever and—"

"Fleming! *Breathe*," Denny says.

"So you don't have to take me, because I can go really fast on my skates. If the parade traffic's bad, I'll be able to pass all the cars. No problem," I tell him as I put on my helmet. "My mother has this crazy idea that I'm never around when she needs me, so I'm going to be there this time."

"It's okay, I get it. You have this need to skate to the rescue. Okay. Whatever," Denny says. "Good luck." He shakes his head.

"Let us know if it's a boy or a girl!" Jamie calls out cheerfully as she goes back into her office and closes the door.

I skate over to the exit. As I'm going out, a man is walking into the store. I hold the door for him and he mumbles a thank-you to me. He looks sort of familiar, but I can't place him. Is he someone I know from the bus? I can't really tell, because he has on a baseball cap and sunglasses. He's probably a tourist, I tell myself. He needs cold beverages, like everyone else. I could use one myself as the blistering hot midday air hits me like a wave.

The door is closing behind me when I hear the guy ask Denny for a couple of scratch tickets. *Wait*, I think. Now I'm sure I know him—his voice is familiar. He has a slight accent, but I can't quite place it. I turn around to look at him one more time. How do I know this guy?

As Denny leans over to pull out the scratch tickets, I see the man reaching in his pocket. Then he holds up a small gun and points it right at Denny.

Oh, my God! It's the c-store robber! I think, and now I really can't breathe at all. I've got to pull it together, I tell myself. I've got to do something.

My body is shaking with nerves but I go back inside as quietly as I can. I glide over to the coffee counter on my skates without making a sound. Jamie is nowhere in sight.

Denny holds up his hands, clutching lottery tickets in each. "So you're the famous robber. Hmm. Interesting."

"Give me all the money in the register," the man says.

I slip behind the counter and grab the first coffee tank pump, then the second. It's a good thing I just made fresh coffee.

"Yeah, okay. But you don't really want to shoot me, do you?" Denny says as he puts the scratch tickets on the counter.

Denny! Just open the register and give him the money! I'm thinking. *We covered this in training!*

"How do you know I don't want to shoot?" the man says. He thrusts the gun toward Denny. "Do it. Now."

I flick the "turbo dispense" button and aim the two coffee tubes at the robber and start shooting coffee at him. My aim isn't good at first and I drench his shoes with coffee, and I hear him mutter, *"Qu'est-ce que c'est?"* Then I turn it on full blast and keep spraying, hitting his legs, his stomach, his throat, and he starts shrieking in pain, singed by Jamie's Java Blend.

Denny rushes around and tackles him to the floor, and I skate over to help. The robber swears in two languages as Denny pulls his arms around and I sit on his back to hold him down.

And now I know why he looks and sounds so familiar. So that's where he's been all summer.

"Monsieur *LeFleur*?" I say. "I was in your class this summer. The one you never showed up to teach because you were too sick and devastated?"

He doesn't say anything.

"*Je m'appelle Mademoiselle Farrell,*" I say. "*Et vous êtes très beaucoup . . .* busted."

"Your accent is terrible," Monsieur LeFleur mutters through gritted teeth.

"Well, whose fault is *that*?" I ask.

Jamie rushes out from the back office carrying a set of handcuffs. "All right, everything's under control," she says.

Denny looks at me and rolls his eyes. "Yeah, thanks to you, Jamie," he says.

"What? I was calling nine-one-one," she says. "*Somebody* had to."

Then we drag LeFleur over to the wall of sodas and handcuff him to one of the fridge door handles.

I say good-bye again and take off skating for the

hospital. I glance at the clock as I'm leaving. It's now just after noon, when I usually catch the bus. I skate in the breakdown lane, and I only get a few blocks before I get to the cars that are completely stopped, held up due to the parade roadblock.

I veer around a dead prairie dog. Then up ahead I see cars pulled over, blocking my way. I glide over and skate on the other side of the stopped cars. No one's moving except me.

I pass the Lindvillager, which is stopped in traffic, not moving at all, looking like a beached battleship.

Then all of a sudden I see this silver car's door opening, and I try to move out of the way, but it's too late. I slam into the door. I feel like I've been cut in half.

You're Kidding, Right?

The next thing I know I am coming to, and there is a cloud of terrible stale coffee air around my head. I'm enveloped in a coffee cloud, and there's no oxygen. I can't breathe. I don't want to breathe.

I open my eyes, and World's Worst Coffee Breath is looming over me. "Look! She's awake! She's going to be just fine, everybody!" He leans down and looks into my eyes. "Are you okay? Can you get up?" he asks cheerfully.

I wince and shake my head, my helmet scratching against the asphalt.

"Sure is a hot one today. Gee, I'm so sorry. What can I do?"

Stop breathing! Eat a Tic Tac! "I have to get to the hospital," I say.

"Really? You're that badly hurt?" Coffee Breath is starting to look very nervous.

"Yes," I say. "But mostly I need to meet my mother

there; she's in labor; I have to help." I try to move, and my right side tells me not to.

I gaze up at the people standing over me like I'm a freak show. I can't believe it, but Kamikaze Driver is here. He's talking with Coffee Breath and gesturing wildly. What did he do, abandon his bus? Why isn't this traffic moving, anyway—is it me?

Then I remember—the parade is going on, and the highway is blocked until the parade finishes passing down Main Street.

I'm hoping Kamikaze won't give me mouth-to-mouth resuscitation, just to give me germs, just to share bacteria. I'm hoping Coffee Breath won't come close enough to even attempt mouth-to-mouth.

Above me, I hear the two of them saying things like "hospital" and "ambulance" and "parade traffic" and "never make it." My body feels cold and clammy, and at the same time the hot black asphalt feels like it's burning through my clothes. I wonder if I'm on my way out. I can't believe I ran into a car door, I can't believe I just did that. Did I really just do that?

Is *this* horrible air—car exhaust being blown on my face, intense heat, feedlot smell—the last breath I'm going to take? That's not fair—none of this is. I'm supposed to be there to help my mother. Maybe she knows how to do everything, but I'm her rock, she said during our last childbirth class—I'm her stationary front. She needs me.

Who else will remind her to pee?

"Can we get going?" I mumble from my prone position on the street.

Coffee Breath and Kamikaze gather me up gingerly. I think I scream a little when they lift me. They carefully put me in the backseat of the silver Lexus and try to prop me in the least painful position. I ask them to take off my helmet, but they refuse, saying we'd better wait until we get to the hospital. Then they both get into the front, and Coffee Breath starts to inch forward in traffic.

"What about . . . the bus?" I ask Kamikaze.

"I told everyone to get off and then I locked it up. Don't worry, nobody's going anywhere in this traffic," Kamikaze says.

"That's the problem!" Coffee Breath says, sounding very tense.

Kamikaze keeps giving him advice, telling him to pass cars, to drive in the wrong direction, against traffic, to drive on the shoulder. Coffee Breath stays in the right lane, hardly moving. They start arguing, louder and louder.

"You think you can do better? You think you can do better?" Coffee Breath asks. "Okay, let's see. Let's switch." He gets out of the car and starts to walk around the back.

Kamikaze slides over to the driver's seat and takes off without him. I hear Coffee Breath screaming behind us as we make an abrupt left and cut between two cars, and it's so tight that the driver's side mirror gets ripped off the car.

I'm not sure if I'm still conscious or not, but I think we're now driving down the wrong side of the street. We're flying, and horns are honking all around us. For a second it feels just like we're cruising on a weekend night because of all the noise.

I try to sit up a little more, and I see that we've reached the roadblock. A mime is standing on top of a sawhorse, walking across the top as if it's a balance beam, trying to amuse all the people in the cars that are backed up for miles.

I glance at Kamikaze. He doesn't look amused.

"There's only one way to get you to the hospital. And you know what it is," he says. I'm not sure if he's talking to me or to himself.

First he jumps out and tries to talk to the mime. The mime makes fun of him, imitates the way he walks.

Kamikaze gets back into the Lexus and nearly runs him over. He pulls past the sawhorse and slyly enters the parade.

I haven't been in the Rodeo Roundup Days parade since fifth grade, when I appeared as a figure skater on the Lindville's Athletes of Tomorrow float. I probably looked better then than I do now. I'm getting blood on the leather upholstery from my cuts.

We weave around the edge of the marching bands, scoot past the square dancers dancing on a truck bed, pass some slowly parading llamas, who get spooked by us and start spitting. Kamikaze finds an open space and blows past some twirlers and jugglers. Then we get stuck, hung up behind a small herd of Longhorn cattle, completely stalled.

"Just one more block and we can cut through the alley to the hospital," Kamikaze tells me. "Just hang in there. What's your name?"

"Coffee Wench," I tell him.

"Pardon?"

"Peggy," I say, and my ribs hurt when I talk. "Fleming."

"Peggy Fleming?" he says, tapping his fingers on the steering wheel. "You're kidding, right?"

"Farrell," I add.

He looks confused and stares at me in the rearview mirror. "What's your name again?"

That's when I hear a motorcycle roar behind us.

"Well, holy cow, would you take a look at this!" Kamikaze cries.

I try to look out the back window. I see Denny on a motorcycle, with a naked girl who's wearing blue-tinted sunglasses and a white cowboy hat. Her long red hair streams out behind her as they zip around us.

Then I black out again.

Web of Evil

"You're in shock, that's all it is, shock," a nurse says to me as I sit on a bed in the emergency room and she checks my vital signs. "You know what it is? You probably haven't eaten a thing today and you drank too much coffee—I know how you kids are."

She's right, but actually I think it was the fact that I was held at gunpoint and then nearly killed, rather than the lack of a balanced breakfast, that makes me keep passing out.

They X-ray my wrist and ribs and make sure nothing is broken, then bind and wrap everything tightly with tape, as if they're trying to hold my bones together just in case they decide to fall apart later. The patches of road burn on my knees, elbows, and palms get doused with antiseptic solution and wrapped in gauze bandages. When the nurse starts talking about whether I should have a tetanus shot, I decide I'd rather pass out again for a while than look at any needles.

The next thing I hear is my father's voice. "We're naming him Elvis," he's saying as he leans over my bed. "For Elvis Stojko. But his middle name's going to be Miles, in case he decides to go by that instead, like his big sister."

"What?" I murmur. I don't know if I'm dreaming this or it's really happening. With my dad and his names, you never know. Miles is my mom's maiden name. Isn't it? They must have given me some medication because I can't quite focus on Dad's mouth, on the words he's saying.

"First we were going with *Scott* because, as you know, we love Scott Hamilton. Then we were convinced we'd pick *Brian*—because of Orser and Boitano. But *then* we considered *Viktor*—for Petrenko—and of course *Alexei*—for Urmanov and Yagudin," my father says.

I don't understand what he's talking about. I don't know why he's speaking in Russian. Has he been studying that with Ludmila, too?

"He's a strong, healthy baby," my father says. "And your mother is doing great."

Unlike me, I think as I look down at the various bandages wrapped around my chest and my legs. But actually, I don't feel all that bad.

"P. F., I'm sorry about our fight," my father says as he sits beside my bed. "I thought about what you said, and I'm going to put off my comeback for another year or so.

Otherwise your senior year will consist of baby-sitting and little else, and your mother will go insane, and I've got to practice what I preach. Who knows? Maybe I'll never do it. It doesn't matter. The point is that I can't tell you to be fiscally responsible when I'm acting like I don't have five children who depend on me."

"You're still young," I say. "And Ludmila thinks you're . . . well, that you've still got it. That you have always had it. So just don't lose it."

"Right," my father says. "P. F., what are you talking about?"

"I don't know," I mumble. "It's Russian. You know Russian."

When the nurse comes to check on me, I tell her I'm okay and ask if I can go see my parents. She insists on having an aide wheel me down the hall to the elevator, even though I can walk, and we go upstairs to the fifth-floor birthing suite. I decide on the way that I have to confess everything.

I work my way up to it, though. I ask my parents about the new baby, and where Torvill, Dean, and Dorothy are. "He's gorgeous, and they're at day care," my mother says.

I look at Elvis, but I can't hold him because my wrist is all wrapped up. I also have two jammed fingers, a couple of bruised ribs, but mostly it's lots and lots of road burn. Hence the mummy look, as my legs are covered in white gauze. My parents won't stop talking about how awful I look, how it must be so painful.

"Come on! Tell me!" I say. "How was the delivery? I mean, talk about pain."

"Five point six for technical merit. Five point nine for presentation," my father says. "Presentation includes your mom screaming at me and asking why I'm not Peggy. 'Where's Peggy, where's Peggy, I need Peggy I mean Fleming where is she!'" He imitates her.

Mom laughs. "I just can't believe—after all our preparations. It must have been one of the fastest deliveries in history." Her face is shiny and at the same time very pale, like she's gone through something incredible but exhausting.

"I'm sorry I missed it," I say. "Well, um, while we're all here, there are some things I have to tell you." I take a deep breath and my ribs hurt. "You're not going to like them, so here goes." I start explaining about borrowing the Shady Prairies golf cart. And how Charlotte and I drove it more than once, and how we also drove it into a pool, and how I went to IHOP that night to confront Steve, and how I've been spending all this time stupidly pursuing him and in the meantime hanging out with his best friend.

While I talk, Mom won't stop crying. "It is sort of sad and pathetic, but it's not *that* bad," I tell her.

"No—that's not it!" She says she can't get over the fact that I got held up by a robber and skated into a car, and she keeps saying it's all her fault.

"It isn't your fault!" I tell her. And then I have to smile, because suddenly I'm remembering everything that's happened in the past few hours. I remember Denny and I busting Monsieur LeFleur; Kamikaze leaving Coffee Breath in the dust, then frightening majorettes into dropping batons, freaking out llamas into spitting, scaring square dancers who missed their do-si-dos; and then being passed by Denny on his motorcycle, with Charlotte, naked, riding in back of him.

"You know who came up to tell us you were here?" my father asks. "This bus driver with a really big beard. He drove you here, I guess, and you told him you had to meet Mom," my father says. "He's a very intense person. I've heard there are complaints about how he drove through the parade, but when everyone heard he was trying to save your life, and that you got hurt by stopping a robbery—"

"But Dad, that's not how I got hurt," I say.

"Yes, I know that, but *they* don't know that. It's one of those stories that got told wrong and it's taken off like wildfire. You're some kind of hero around Lindville now, and so is that bus driver. It's good publicity. Ride it for a while," my father says.

"Okay," I agree. "But I'm still sorry about the golf cart, you guys. And I'm sorry if I've had a bad attitude. It's just . . . staying here this summer, without a car . . . I feel so trapped sometimes. Like you know the way the air here gets at night after a hot day, and it just feels like the air's really bad and it's just sort of sitting on top of you? And smelling?"

My mother nods. "It's called inversion."

"Inversion, then. That's sort of my life right now," I say.

My father looks at me. "Is it that bad?"

"No. Well, sometimes," I admit. "I mean, there are all the changes we talked about. We used to have kind of exciting lives, you know? And now . . . I mean, I love Dean and Torvill and Dorothy, so much. But couldn't I love them in New York or L.A. or somewhere fun?"

"But this is our home now," my mother says slowly, as if I'm the baby. "We can't move."

"I know. I know that," I say.

"But you were right—what you said last night. We've been taking advantage of you," Mom says. "I'm going to quit asking you to do so much stuff around the house. You're just so capable that I kept adding on without realizing—you're sixteen. You have your own life. You shouldn't be home on Saturday nights—you should be on a date. I know *I* would have been."

Dad looks at her a little sharply, alarmed by this news.

I smile. "The thing is, I might not be able to actually get a date. Anytime soon."

"Who cares about dates?" my father says, looking a little happier now. "Friends, then. Maybe I don't like the

Plot and the Lot and the whatever comes up next . . . the Cot . . . wait, forget I said that . . . anyway, I know you well enough to trust you. You might not be the best driver, okay. But we can work on that."

"Really? So does that mean I could maybe start driving again soon? Not right away—I know I still owe you money, so I'll pay that back first. But at the end of the summer, or when I turn seventeen, in November? I could buy an old car, or borrow one of yours once in a while?"

"Yes," my mother says. "Of course."

"You know, I thought of giving you back your license yesterday, actually," my father says. "Just in case you needed to drive Mom to the hospital. But I actually couldn't *find* your license. I don't know what I did with it. It's in my desk somewhere, but things have been so hectic. . . ."

I smile. That fits in with everything else lately. I have my license back, but I don't have an actual license.

Which is okay, because I don't have an actual car.

Which is okay, because I can't really drive right now, because of my bandaged body.

"But P. F. About the golf cart," my father says. "You'll need to call Shady Prairies when we get home and tell them what you did. And let them decide what action to take."

"Right. I know," I say.

"And we're going to have more driving lessons, you and me. A lot more. Remember how intense I was about your skating a few years ago? Like that."

"Four hours a *day*?" I ask.

"Sure. In very, very short shifts. Lots of errands. Driving Elvis around until he falls asleep—things like that." He glances at my mother, who's rubbing Elvis's tiny fingers. "And once a week you can practice highway driving by taking me to the arena to skate. Maybe. If it's convenient for your mother."

"We'll see," she says. "Torvill and Dean will be in kindergarten, so . . ." She lets out a deep sigh. Suddenly her eyes are brimming over with tears. She opens her mouth to talk, but she can't. Dad gives her a hug, being careful to leave enough room for Elvis between them.

I ask an aide to wheel me out of the room into the hallway to give them some privacy. She parks me just outside the door so they won't have to look far for me.

Charlotte and Denny come to the hospital at about 5:30, just as my dad is preparing to take me home. They heard about my accident when Coffee Breath showed up at Gas 'n Git, looking for a phone. Charlotte's called three times already to check on me and see when I'm being released. Denny doesn't come inside, but I can see him through the sliding glass doors, perched on his bike. He waves at me and blows me a kiss, like he's the one on parade now.

Charlotte rushes up to the admissions desk and is

about to throw her arms around me when she notices my bandages. "Fleming! I can't believe you!" she says. "You saved Denny's life!"

"I did?" I ask.

"Yes! *And* you took out that idiot LeFleur."

"So what about you?" I say. "Did I see what I think I saw?" I'm talking nonsense again. I haven't been able to speak clearly all day.

"Charlotte? What did you do?" my father asks, turning around from filling out some insurance paperwork.

"Just rode a motorcycle, that's all," Charlotte says, smiling at him.

"So it *was* you I heard about," my father says. He turns to me. "Wild streak. Emphasis on *streak*. Okay? I told you, P. F." He starts laughing and Charlotte's face turns nearly as red as her hair.

When my father turns back to the desk, Charlotte says quietly, "So I saw Mike and Steve after the parade, and they both asked about you, and I told them about the robber thing and they were both *so* impressed and worried about you. So. Which one do you like?"

"I don't know," I say. I think about it for a couple of seconds. "Neither, I guess."

"Really?" she asks.

"Really."

"Oh. Well, okay. We'll find a new FEN for you, then."

"What's a FEN?" my father wants to know as he

comes back toward us.

"You know, Fleming, you look sort of terrible," Charlotte says, deftly changing the subject. "Let me come over tonight and fix you up."

"How exactly are you going to get to our house?" my father asks her with a critical stare. "Do you need a ride, or were you just going to . . . hmm, I don't know. Jump-start a golf cart?"

"Denny will drive me, of course, Mr. Farrell." Charlotte smiles nervously.

"Good answer," my father says. "I think."

That night, while Charlotte's painting my toenails blue to match my taped wrist, we see Monsieur LeFleur on the 9:00 TV news. The theory is that he will plead not guilty by reason of temporary insanity. This doesn't make sense to me because his insanity—otherwise known as a stealing spree—lasted a few weeks, at least.

His written statement says that he devoted his whole life to teaching, lost his wife over it, and never made enough to live on. That's why he cracked. Extreme burnout. It could make anyone into an armed robber of convenience stores.

"Do you realize what this means?" Charlotte says. "They're going to *have* to pass us all now. With As."

"Even if we didn't really learn that much?" I say.

"It's a public relations nightmare for the school," she

says. "Their best teacher is a criminal. They'll do *anything* to get us to be quiet."

"But he was never there," I remind her. "We never had any contact with him."

"We didn't, but *you* did," Charlotte says. "He had a gun, Fleming."

"It wasn't a real gun. It turned out to be a toy," I say.

"So what? He was still dangerous. Very dangerous. He could have affected us somehow, drawn us into his web of evil," Charlotte says. "Without us even knowing it. He could have been controlling us with his homework assignments."

I start laughing. "Oh, yeah, definitely," I agree.

"And if he ever *had* shown up, he probably would have taken us hostage or something, and demanded a ransom." She laughs. "We'll point all this out if they try to give us *B*s. *And* we'll mention how he put your life at risk, and how you saved Denny's life."

"And how the subs were so bad that we want a refund!" I cry, pounding my fist on top of the coffee table. For a second I picture Kamikaze Driver demanding free coffee, and our "free ride" conversation. I'll have to find him and thank him for bringing me to the hospital. I still don't know his name, but I do know his route. "You know, all this stuff with Monsieur LeFleur is the most I've ever done just to get an *A*," I tell Charlotte.

"I've never *gotten* an *A* before," she admits, and we

start laughing so hard that she paints the rug with blue nail polish.

Fortunately, it blends in with the stain from the last time Dean spilled grape juice.

Because I Really Like Pink

It's noon on Torvill and Dean's birthday, and I'm standing by the main entrance at Shady Prairies, waiting for my father to pick me up. I just got out of my brand-new job. Starting today, I'm teaching water exercise as part of my community service, to pay back Shady Prairies for stealing a golf cart and then flipping it into their pool. Until I go back to work at Gas 'n Git, where there's now a plaque on the wall naming me and Denny "Employees of the Month," I'll be here swimming with seniors. My hair now smells like chlorine, but other than that, it wasn't bad at all. I can definitely do this for two weeks, especially since Jamie insisted I take some time off.

Charlotte has to work the breakfast shift now instead of dinner, because the people in Shady Prairies' personnel department know how much she hates mornings. She got it much worse than me, because they trusted her and she let them down. Also because she admitted that traveling "à la cart" was her idea, and that she was the one who drove. She also has to clean the pool and "maintain" the bathroom by the pool.

I hear a rumble of thunder above me and glance up at the sky. I see some dark clouds building in the west. It looks like we might get a storm later. I may not be Christie Farrell from KLDV, and I'm no link to Mother Nature, but I think I see something heading our way. I hope it doesn't ruin Torvill and Dean's birthday party.

I hear a car honk and am amazed to see my father pulling up. He's actually on time. This is . . . unheard of.

Later that afternoon I am walking across our backyard carrying a giant Gabe's Auto World cup of cold water for my mom. The thermometer says it is ninety-seven degrees, but it feels hotter. It's the sixth day in a row where it's been over ninety-five.

There are twenty five-year-olds and one three-year-old, Dorothy, sprinting back and forth across our lawn, chasing each other all over. Grass is flying up from their sneakers.

I tried to kick off the party with a quiet little game of pin the tail on the donkey. Then Dean pinned the tail on Torvill. She turned around and started chasing him, and suddenly it turned into a giant game of free-form tag, where everybody seems to be "it." Dean's wearing the cowboy hat I gave him for his birthday, only it keeps flying off his head. Torvill hid the little suede change purse I gave her in her room—which means she'll probably never find it again.

Mom is sitting in a chaise longue under an umbrella, with Elvis in a little sack snuggled against her chest. Dad is chasing the kids around with a pitcher of lemonade and making sure that they all get enough to drink, so they don't get dehydrated.

As I set the glass of ice water down next to my mom, I notice a car coming up the cul-de-sac. There's smoke coming out of it. The motor dies and the car coasts up to our house. I notice that it's a rusted yellow Geo Metro. *No*, I think. *It can't be.* Then the door opens and Mike gets out, cursing and kicking the car.

Of all the pizza places to call in Lindville, Mom had to call Smiley's? I really don't feel like seeing Mike right now. I have multiple bandages on my legs. I also have a party hat on my head and three colors of frosting smeared on my shirt. I don't know why it still matters what I look like to Mike, but it does. Not because it could get back to Steve, but because the last time I saw Mike didn't exactly go well. I owe him an apology, and I don't want to do it wearing a pointed pink hat with a 5 on it.

Mike lifts the hood and props it open, using the bottom of his T-shirt like a potholder. Steam billows out and nearly engulfs his head. He jumps back, coughing and wiping his face. Like Denny said, Mike's not the crispest crisp in the chip bucket, although he was almost pretty crispy there for a second.

He grabs his delivery sheet to check the address. Then he reaches into the backseat and pulls out a giant stack of pizzas. He doesn't seem to have noticed that it's me or my house yet as he trudges up the driveway in his flip-flops.

"Farrell residence? Christie Farrell?" Mike asks, standing cluelessly in front of me. He can't really see over the top of the stack of pizza boxes.

"Right," I say, sliding the party hat off my head. "Could you come set them down over here, on the picnic table?"

He clears his throat and follows me. When he sets down the pizzas and looks at me, his face is beaded with sweat. He opens his mouth to say something, then stops. Then he says, "Hey."

"Hi," I say.

He peers around me at Dorothy, who is now clinging to my leg. This is extremely awkward.

"So how are you?" I ask him.

"Hot." Mike mops his forehead with his sleeve. "And my car overheated."

"Sorry." I nod, feeling like a complete idiot. I don't know what to say to him, but it has to be something besides "sorry" and "how are you." We spent half the summer hanging out. We melded in a car wash once.

277

"So it's sixty-eight dollars," he says.

I stare at the wad of cash in my hands. My father had forgotten he needed to go get cash, so he spent the morning flattening dollar bills that had been stuffed into the "cloudy day" jar. "This should be eighty," I say as I hand the clump of ones to Mike.

"Oh. Yeah?" He finally smiles and runs his hands through his sweat-soaked hair and I look at his cheekbones and black T-shirt and for a second remember why I was attracted to him. "That's great."

"No problem. I mean, it's my parents, so . . . I mean, it's not like I have any money, so . . ." Dorothy tugs on my leg again, as if even she can tell I am blowing this. "So, Mike. Sorry about what happened that night. I shouldn't have yelled at you. I guess I just overreacted, but I didn't mean to take it out on you."

Mike dodges a couple of racing kids who nearly slam into his leg. "It's okay," he says. "I mean, I know you and Gropher . . . whatever. I actually don't know."

"Yeah. Me neither," I admit with a laugh. Mike's summary seems pretty accurate.

"Hey, do you think you could maybe give me a ride back to work?" he asks.

"I can't, but my dad could, right after the cake."

"Yeah, okay." Mike sighs and sits down at the picnic table. "It's too hot to work, anyway. "You got anything to drink?"

"Lem'nade," Dorothy says, and hands him an empty cup. She points to the folding table by the house.

"Thanks," Mike tells her with a nice smile. "I'll get some." He gets up. "Is it pink?"

Dorothy shakes her head.

"Oh. Because I really like pink," he says, disappointed. He turns to walk across the lawn.

As I watch him, I can't quite believe we almost sort of went out. Even though it might not count because I was using him to get to Steve and that makes me a very bad person. But I'll never do that again, not to anyone. And definitely not to impress Steve Gropher, or anyone else. For some reason, I really don't care about impressing anyone anymore.

Dorothy looks up at me. "P. F. okay? Need lem'nade?"

"No, I'm good," I tell her.

"Attention, everyone, attention!" Dad says, clapping his hands above his head. He blows a whistle to get the kids to stop racing around. "We've got pizza! Kids! Sit down, please!"

Dad helps gather Torvill and Dean, and the kids suddenly drop onto the lawn under a tree, desperate for shade. Another parent grabs several pizzas and brings them over to the group.

I seek shelter under the umbrella with Elvis and Mom, both of whom have fallen asleep. I crouch beside Mom's chair and gently rub Elvis's fuzzy head. I hold my hand out and feel warm drops of water spitting from the sky.

Mom is instantly awake. "Rain. Of course," she says, as rain taps on the canvas umbrella. "I felt it coming. It won't last long, though. Don't worry, Fleming," she tells me.

And she's right, because almost as soon as it's started, it stops.

"Peggy, I'm a cowboy!" Dean yells as he races past me carrying Torvill's new stick horse, pretending to gallop. His cowboy hat flies off his head and lands on the ground.

"*I'm* a cowboy!" Torvill cries, chasing him. "Give me back my horsey!"

I pick up Dean's hat just as Dad comes over to me. I set it on my head, and he smiles. "Hey, thanks for all your help today."

"No problem," I say, fixing the clasp on the stretchy ACE bandage around my wrist. When I went in for a follow-up appointment, the doctor removed the tape, because it's healing so quickly.

Dad points to it. "How's the wrist? Not bothering you, is it?"

"Not at all. It feels totally fine," I say. "In fact, I almost feel ready to get back to my old routine."

"You mean, going back to work at Gas 'n Git? Or what are you saying?"

"Any second now, it's all going to come together," I say.

Dad looks confused. "What?"

"Clouds, silver linings. Sacrifices. You know."

"P. F., you don't sound like yourself. Make sure you drink plenty of water, okay?" Dad shakes his head and walks away, convinced I'm dehydrated.

I just smile and go over to sit with Mike.

Do Not Adjust Your Sets

It's the final night of Rodeo Roundup Days. The heat has broken after a cold front came in the night before, bringing strong winds, occasional thunder and lightning, and heavy rain. The cooler temperature is good for keeping the ice frozen, but bad for the other events. The final bull-riding challenge was canceled because the arena's too muddy, the petting zoo has closed early, and the rides are all closed due to risk of lightning strikes. The wind is rattling the chain-link fence, and the boards sound as if they might fly off.

But the skating cowboy show must go on. So I'm standing here at the end of the rink, waiting with everyone else for the 7:00 show.

There's a strong gust of wind, and I smell a slightly manly lavender and oatmeal fragrance blowing through the air. It's familiar to me, but I can't quite place it. I turn to my right and see Mr. Stinson standing right next to me.

"He's quite good, your father," Mr. Stinson says. "I've been here almost every night, and he's quite consistent."

"Yes, he is. I told you he wouldn't let you down, didn't I?" I say.

"Yes. It's a shame he's decided not to go for that tour after all," Mr. Stinson says. "I'd have sponsored him for sure."

"Well, maybe another time," I say.

"Right. Or perhaps I'll sponsor a show here—I've been thinking about asking him to skate a special Christmas show." There's an awkward pause as we both think back to last Christmas. Then he steps a little closer to me. "It's ironic, don't you think?"

I turn toward him. "What is?" I ask. Or maybe I should ask, *What isn't?*

"Your encounter with the robber," Mr. Stinson says. "It's ironic that you would be the one to dispense justice, after your own checkered past." He makes me sound like a convicted felon, as if I were in a work-release program. Or maybe that's just how I feel. "But I suppose you have a right to evolve as much as the next person."

Evolve. Is that what I've been doing? "I'm not a bad seed, and I'm not evil. Is that what you're saying?" I ask him.

He almost smiles. "I suppose you simply needed to find the right employment. The right outlet for your talents. And lucky for you that you have. Selling petrol is a noble profession."

"I don't actually have anything to do with . . . petrol,"
I say. "I make the coffee. Sometimes tea. I'm good at picking up muffins with tongs."

"Ah. Well. No matter. It's a shame that ungrateful
excuse for a French teacher got the best of you. French.
What did we expect," he complains, shaking his head.

"*He's* not French," I say. "He only *taught* French.
Anyway, it was a car door that really got me."

"Yes. Well, not to worry. You're young; you'll heal."
He slaps me on the back, so hard that I can feel it in my
ribs.

It hurts, but I'm not going to let it stop me tonight.
And since Mr. Stinson apparently doesn't hate me any-
more, I have a question. "Can I ask you something, Mr.
Stinson?" I say.

"I suppose," he says, somewhat grudgingly.

"When you moved here to Lindville, however many
years ago, why did you do it?" I ask. "I've always won-
dered. What made you stay?"

"I had an excellent business opportunity, a great
chance to invest in—oh, look," Mr Stinson sighs as he
unsnaps his heavy yellow rain slicker. For once, the
weather actually suits his outfit. "I came to America
because I wanted a cattle ranch, all right? That's why I
came here to Lindville. That's why I'm still here."

I hate to state the obvious. "But you don't have a

ranch," I say. The last I knew, Mr. Stinson lived in a large ranch *house*, in our general neighborhood. "Do you?"

"Yes, I know. I'm well *aware* of that." He pushed his glasses up on his nose, the frames mashing his bushy eyebrows. "However, I will someday. I'm not giving up yet. In the meantime I have my shop, and life is not too hard to take around here, now, is it?"

I don't say anything. A month ago, I would have said "Actually, *yes*, it is," without even hesitating. But now, I'm not so sure. Maybe I'm not going anywhere in a hurry, either.

At 6:59 there's a crackle over the loudspeaker. Then a voice says, "Attention, ladies and gentlemen. There has been a slight change in tonight's program. Do not adjust your sets."

I watch my father's face as he steps out of the warm-up room and peers at the hockey penalty box that's being used as an audio booth.

Denny looks out and waves at him. "I repeat, ladies and gentlemen, do not adjust your sets," Denny says in a deep voice. Then he smiles and starts playing the music that begins Dad's program.

"Excuse me," I say to Mr. Stinson. "Would you mind holding this for a second?" I take off my coat and hand it to him, then lean over to retie my laces and pick up Charlotte's hat.

When I straighten up, Mr. Stinson is staring at my

outfit: a vintage pale green Western-style shirt I found at the thrift shop two days ago, a pair of boot-cut stretch jeans with a black belt, and my new silver PFF belt buckle. I pull the white hat over my hair, which is in two braids. Mr. Stinson looks down at my feet and for the first time realizes that I'm not wearing shoes.

"What on earth . . ." he mutters as I slip the rubber guards off my white figure skates. "Miss Farrell? What's the meaning of this?"

My father skates to center ice and suddenly his usual country music comes to an abrupt end. He looks over at Denny, confused. He stares at me as I open the side door and glide onto the ice. I skate toward him and stop with a flourish, spraying him with ice flakes. He looks like he's going to faint. I don't know who's more surprised at the fact I'm doing this, Dad or me.

"Ladies and gentlemen, presenting Phil and Fleming Farrell in, uh, 'Cowboy' . . . 'Cowgirl' . . . oh, forget the title. Here they are, so start clapping, already!"

The audience applauds politely, looking confused as Charlotte drags a few small hay bales over to the sides of the rink. As arranged, the rodeo clowns gently lead the lambs and horses off the ice to make room for us. I asked for their help when I first came down to practice a few days ago.

"You won't need this," I say, taking the rope lariat from Dad and tossing it aside.

As the opening notes of U2's "Who's Gonna Ride Your Wild Horses" play over the loudspeaker, my dad says out of the corner of his mouth, "P. F.? Are you sure about this?"

"No," I admit.

"What are we going to do?" my father asks as we push off and start to circle the rink, to the sound of Bono's voice.

"We'll wing it," I say as we both turn and start skating backward. "Just like we used to."

Don't miss the newest summer romance from

CATHERINE CLARK

Turn the page for a sneak peek!

I can't *wait* to see all the guys."

You might have thought that was me talking, as I headed into the town of Kill Devil Hills, North Carolina, my destination for a two-week summer stay on the Outer Banks.

But no. It was my dad, of all people.

And it's not what you might be thinking *now*, either. He was talking about seeing his best friends from college.

We meet up every few years on a big reunion trip with "the guys," their wives, their kids, and other assorted members of their families—dogs, parents, random cousins, nannies, you name it. I think it's Dad's favorite vacation, because he and his buddies play golf, sit around reminiscing, and stay up late talking every night.

Even though that occasionally gets a little boring, I

like going on these trips, because I've gotten to be friends with "the guys'" offspring, who have sprung off like me: Heather Olsen, Adam Thompson, and Spencer Flanagan. I couldn't wait to see all of them. It had been two years since the last vacation reunion for the four of us, which was *almost*, but not quite, long enough to make me forget what an idiot I'd made of myself the last time, when I was fifteen, Spencer was sixteen, and I'd told him that I thought he was really cool and that we really clicked and that I wished we lived closer because then we could . . . well, you get the gist. *Embarrassing*. With a capital *E*. Maybe three of them, in fact. EEEmbarrassing. Like an extra-wide foot that I'd stuck in my mouth.

But enough about me and my slipup. I basically love these trips because we end up in cool locations like this, a place I'd never seen, or even gotten close to seeing, before now. Living in the Midwest, we don't get to the coast much.

"This is just *beautiful*," Mom said as we turned off the main four-lane road, and onto a smaller road with giant three- and four-story beach houses on each side of it.

We were getting close to the house number we were looking for when Dad stopped the car as two college-age-looking guys stepped out to cross the street. They had beach towels slung around their necks and bare chests with nice abs, and wore low-riding surf shorts. One of them carried a Frisbee, while another had a volleyball tucked under his arm.

I sat up in the backseat, wondering if that was Adam and Spencer. But no, upon closer inspection, one of them had short, nearly platinum-blond hair, and the other's was brown, shoulder-length—not at all like Spencer and Adam.

Which wasn't a bad thing, because I was looking forward to seeing what guys might be around, too. And I *didn't* mean Dad's college buddies or their sons.

While we were stopped, the guy carrying the volleyball leaned down and peered into the car—I guess he'd caught me staring at him. He smiled at me, then waved with a casual salute.

I smiled and waved back to him. I wanted to take a lot of pictures on this trip, so why not start now? I buzzed the window down. "Hold on a second, okay?" I asked. I grabbed my slim, shiny green camera from my bag, and took some quick shots as they played along, grinning and flexing their muscles, showing off a couple of tattoos.

"Emily." My mother peered over the front seat. "What are you doing?"

"Capturing the local flavor," I said as a car behind us honked its horn, and the guys hustled across the street so we could get moving again.

"Hmph," my mother said, while my dad laughed.

I turned around and looked out the back window at the guys, wondering if we'd be staying anywhere close by, when Mom shrieked, "Look! There's the house!"

Dad parked the car with a screech of the brakes and we started to climb out. I closed the door and I swear, a piece of the car fell off onto the pavement.

There was a second or two where I was dreading the inevitable hugging and screaming that went along with greeting everyone. Then the back door opened, I saw Adam's dad, and the feeling was over.

"Jay, you could have at least rented a decent car for once in your life," Mr. Thompson said.

"Why change now?" my dad replied as he clapped him on the back.

"Once a cheapskate, always a cheapskate, huh, Emily?" Mr. Thompson gave me a little shoulder hug.

"Don't get me started," I mumbled, looking up at him with a smile.

"Adam just took off on a run down the beach," Mr. Thompson said. "Heather and her mom are off shopping somewhere. I know Adam is psyched to see you."

"Cool." I grinned. After that long car ride with my parents, I had to figure out where the people my actual age had hidden themselves.

As they say on *Grey's Anatomy*? *Stat.*

❖ ❖ ❖

4

Ten minutes later, after dumping my suitcase in my room, I stood on the giant back deck, overlooking the ocean. There were houses up and down the beach, all looking pretty similar. On one side of us there seemed to be a large, extended family, complete with lots of young kids, grandparents, and about a dozen beach balls and other water toys floating in their pool.

The house on the other side of us had beach towels lined up on the deck railing, flapping in the warm breeze, a couple of lacrosse sticks, a random collection of Frisbees and badminton racquets strewn on the deck, along with a cooler and some empty cans of Red Bull and bottles of sports drink.

Down by the ocean, some kids were playing in the sand, building sand castles and moats, while others swam and tried to ride waves on boogie boards.

"I've made a list of the top ten Outer Banks destinations. I read eight different guidebooks and compiled my own list," my mom was explaining to Mrs. Thompson when I walked over to them. "We'll need to go food shopping tonight, of course, and make a schedule for who cooks which night."

"Oh, relax, you can do the shopping tomorrow. Things are very casual around here," Mrs. Thompson said to her. "Dinner's already on the grill, put your feet up." She turned to me. "You should go say hi to Adam. He's down there, in the water."

"He is?"

She gestured for me to join her at the edge of the deck. "He's right there. Don't you see him?"

All I could see except for young kids was a man with large shoulders doing the crawl, his arms powerfully slicing through the water. "That?" I coughed. "That person is Adam?"

His stepmom nodded. "Of course."

Wow. Really? I wanted to say. When I focused on him again, as he strode out of the surf, I nearly dropped my camera over the railing and into the sand. "You know what? I think I *will* go say hi." *Hi, and who are you, and what have you done with my formerly semi-wimpy friend?*

I walked down the steps to the beach in disbelief. Last time I'd seen Adam, his voice was squeaking, and he was on the scrawny side—a wrestler at one of the lower weights, like 145. Not anymore. He had muscular arms and shoulders, and he looked about a foot taller than he had two years ago. His curly brown hair was cut short.

You look different, I wanted to say, but that would be dumb. *You look different and I sound like an idiot, so really, nothing's changed.*

Why was it that whenever I tried to talk to a guy, I started speaking a completely different language? Stupidese?

"Emily?" he asked.

I nodded, noticing that his voice was slightly deeper than I remembered it. It was sort of like he'd gone into a time machine and come out in the future, whereas I felt exactly the same. "Hi."

He leaned back into the surf to wet his hair. "You look different," he said when he stood up.

"Oh, yeah? I do?" *Different how?* I wanted to ask, but that was potentially embarrassing. Different in the way he did? Like . . . sexy? I waited for him to elaborate, but he didn't. "Well, uh, you do, too," I said.

"Right." He smiled, then picked up his towel and dried his hair. As he had the towel over his head, I took the opportunity to check him out again. Man. What a difference a couple years could make. He used to wear wire-rim glasses, but now, apparently, he had contacts, like me.

There was always this really uncomfortable moment when we first tried to talk after not having seen each other for so long.

"So, how are you?" I asked, patting his shoulder, and then we sort of hugged, very awkwardly, the way you hug someone without actually touching them. Sort of like the Hollywood fake-kiss.

"All right, knock it off, you two!" a voice said.

Funny—that didn't *sound* like my mother, but who else would care if I hugged a suddenly semi-hot Adam?

7

Chapter 2

I turned to look at who was coming toward us, but the sun was in my eyes.

"You guys!" Heather Olsen cried. "It's *me*." She had on a pair of short shorts and a couple of layered tank tops. She ran up to us, and I gave her a big hug, squeezing her tightly.

"Yay, you're here!" I said. "I haven't seen you in forever."

"I know. Isn't it ridiculous, considering how close we live?" she replied.

I gave her another hug, because the last time we'd gotten together wasn't for a vacation—it was for her dad's memorial service nearly a year ago. We hadn't visited much that time, but we'd stayed in close touch throughout the past year with emails. The guys hadn't come to the service, only their parents had, because they now lived pretty far away—Adam and his family lived in Oregon, while Spencer's was in Vermont. Emily and I were the ones still sort of near where everyone started out—Madison, Wisconsin, where they'd all moved and rented a house together *after* college and gone to grad school. We still lived in Madison, while Heather and her mom lived in Chicago, which was only about three hours away. Still, we were usually both so busy we didn't see each other often enough.

"What are you—" Adam asked as Heather jumped on his back, like she wanted a piggy-back ride. "I wasn't sure you were coming," he said when she dropped off his back and gave him a playful shove.

"Why wouldn't I?" Heather stared at him, hands on her hips. "No. Only kidding. I know why. But the other guys put on the major hard sell, or maybe it was a guilt trip. Anyway, Mom finally agreed. I told her I wanted to see you guys."

"I'm really glad you came," I told her. "It wouldn't be the same, you know. Without you." I felt myself tripping over my tongue. "Right, Adam?"

"Definitely." Adam looked up at a few pelicans flying past. "It wouldn't count as a reunion."

"We have traditions," I said. "You know. You and Spencer make fun of me and Heather until you run out of put-downs, then you resort to practical jokes."

"Me?" Adam turned to me, not looking amused. "No, I don't."

9

"You do," I said.

"It's a good thing I'm here, because Emily couldn't possibly defend herself on her own, right?" Heather said.

"What? I could too defend myself," I said. I put up my fists, which aren't all that impressive, actually, considering my arms have this certain resemblance to sticks. All the muscle tone I'd had from ballet over the years had started to fizzle, like the deflating air mattress I'd been forced to sleep on the night before at my aunt and uncle's, who live close to the airport.

"Yeah, but not *well*." Heather punched Adam lightly on the arm, which was no longer an arm but a massive bicep. She rubbed her knuckles afterward and looked up at him. "Speaking of self-defense. Work out much?"

"Yeah." He shrugged. "I just finished baseball season."

"I thought they banned steroids in baseball," Heather said.

Adam laughed, looking slightly embarrassed. "Shut up."

"Fine. You know what? I'm starved. When do we eat? I think I saw some brats on the grill."

"What else is new?" I asked, rolling my eyes. "Cheddar or beer style?"

"You can take my dad out of Wisconsin, but you

can't take his bratwurst away," Adam said.

Heather started to run back up the stairs to the deck, then she stopped and looked over her shoulder. "Well, come on, guys, I'm not going to eat by myself."

"We're coming," I told her.

"I forgot how she is," Adam commented as we walked over to the stairs together, me loving the feeling of digging my toes into the soft, warm sand. "I mean, maybe it's a good thing she hasn't changed, with everything that's happened."

"How is she?" I asked.

"Like, um, a whirling dervish," Adam said. "Those things that spin around and around."

"Whirling dervish? Wow, have you been taking vocab vitamins along with your steroids?" I asked.

"Shut up." He gave me a playful—but still possibly bruising, with his strength—hip check as we headed up to the deck. "I don't take steroids, okay? I mean, I know guys who've done it and it's disgusting. So let's not talk about that anymore," Adam said in a more serious tone.

"Agreed," I said. "I didn't really think that, you know." Although it had kind of crossed my mind, because I didn't understand how he'd transformed himself. If he'd changed that much . . . what would Spencer look like? "Anyway, let's forget we ever said anything, and just eat."

"Deal." Adam picked up a paper plate and started loading it with food. I followed his lead, taking some of almost everything.

Heather and I sat next to each other on the deck. We both sat cross-legged, in a sort of yoga position. She's tiny—about five feet tall—and used to do gymnastics at the same level I danced—we were both a little obsessed. She'd always been amazingly flexible, and I was, too, so we used to spend these vacations trying to out-bend each other doing splits, back bends, handstands, and anything else we could do to be pretzelesque. Adam and Spencer had dubbed us the tumbling twins—or maybe it was the tumbling twits. I suddenly couldn't remember.

Maybe there were some things about our last gettogether that I'd purposely forgotten, like the look on Spencer's face when I'd awkwardly tried to tell him how I felt—or the look of his back, rather, when he turned away, ignoring me, as if I hadn't said anything. A person can forget a lot in two years. But that? No. And if I hadn't forgotten, I worried he hadn't, either.

Maybe the Flanagans won't come, I thought, looking around at everyone else already gathered. Maybe they decided to stay home. Maybe their car broke down and they'd decided to just can it.

Oh, relax, I told myself as I bit into a cob of buttery corn. *Spencer has moved on, and so have you. You've had tons of other guys in your life since then. Sure. There's that tech guy at the Apple store . . . and the guy at the Starbucks drive-through you flirted with — once — and . . . um . . .*

Adam sat down across from us. "What's wrong with chairs, anyway? You guys against chairs? Wait, I know. You have to stretch. Isn't that what you were always doing?"

"Before I quit gymnastics," Heather said. "Actually, I just didn't see enough chairs."

"When did you quit gymnastics?" Adam asked, sounding genuinely surprised.

"After the accident," she said. "I broke a few ribs, and . . . it hurt to breathe, never mind flip. Plus I was just ready to make some changes."

Adam nodded. "Yeah. Sorry about that. I mean . . . about everything. Must have been really hard."

There was a long pause. I looked at Adam, then at Heather, then at my plate, wishing I could say something decent that didn't sound completely clichéd.

"You know what?" Heather suddenly looked up at both of us and smiled. "We have to go out tonight."

"We do?" I asked. I hadn't pictured going out and partying as being in the cards, not with the proportion of parents to us. I mean, it was something I'd hoped to achieve, but only in a fantasy, which is the way most of my daring plans occur.

Icing on the Lake

Kirsten's New Year's resolution is to find a hockey-playing, winter-loving hottie to invite to her weekend cabin. No problem...right?

Maine Squeeze

Living on a tiny island off the coast of Maine is boring, right? Not when you have a great new boyfriend...and then last summer's boyfriend unexpectedly comes to town!

So Inn Love

Liza has finally landed her dream job at the Tides Inn on the Rhode Island shore. Now she just needs to figure out a way to get in with the in crowd.

Wish You Were Here

Ariel is stuck on an "America's Heartland" bus tour with her family for four weeks! But then she meets intriguing, also-miserable Andre. Who has a plan to escape.

HARPER TEEN
An Imprint of HarperCollins Publishers

www.harperteen.com